DIRECT DEPOSIT

Marilyn Baxter

www.BOROUGHSPUBLISHINGGROUP.com

DIRECT DEPOSIT
Copyright © 2015 Marilyn Puett

ISBN 978-1-941260-95-1

To my sister Bev. Even though she's a CPA, she is quite good with spelling and grammar. She also knows the US tax codes inside and out while I only understand one thing about taxes: I have to pay them. She stuck with me long-distance via email through NaNoWriMo when I wrote the first draft of this book. Her daily first draft proofreading, knowledge of the Atlanta area and endless encouragement kept me writing 1667 words every day for thirty days. I still remember the fun we had meeting in Atlanta and going to all the places I used for inspiration in the book—the Georgian Terrace and Biltmore hotels, the now-defunct Agnes & Muriel's restaurant, the house in Virginia Highlands I used as inspiration for my heroine's home and Tiffany & Company. And who can forget hot dogs and peach fried pies at the Varsity? Let's do a book inspiration trip again, only let's set the book in...oh, what the heck, Europe!

ACKNOWLEDGMENTS

To Roxanne St. Claire, who uttered six words that sent a shiver down my spine, clicked on the light bulb in my head and sent this story in the right direction. "What if he was her husband?" Those words still make me shiver.

And to Susan Crosby, who asked me to join her at lunch at my very first RWA conference when I stood at the door to the hotel ballroom evidently looking as lost as I felt. A number of conferences later, over lunch away from the hotel, she helped me see the story's resolution by pointing out the obvious, which I often don't see.

Thank you both for your help, your support and your continued friendship.

CONTENTS

DIRECT DEPOSIT

One

Your sperm canister will be shipped and…

The folded white paper tucked behind the wall phone contrasted brightly against the red brick kitchen and all but begged to be read. Those words were like a magnet. He knew he should respect his hostess's privacy, but Jack Worth believed a deathbed promise created loopholes in the confidentiality laws that made it okay to read Maddie Prescott's mail.

Jack winced mentally at his creative interpretation of that law, especially since Maddie was an attorney. He'd spent too many years wobbling along the line between good and bad, and, once he'd been pulled back from the Dark Side, he rather enjoyed the benefits associated with being a law-abiding citizen.

The few words of text he could read indicated the canister would be shipped by overnight delivery. Without pulling the paper from its place, Jack had no way to be sure when the item in question would be shipped or to whom.

Maddie's specialty was family law so this could be in relation to one of her clients, but it seemed odd to stick a notification behind her phone and not put it in a client file. Maddie followed the law to the letter and she'd never leave confidential information lying about at home, especially sticking an important document behind the kitchen phone in full view. This was unlike her. She was so organized her spices were alphabetized and her grocery lists correlated to the aisles in the store.

Or, perhaps she was going to do something crazy. And the prevention of craziness was his responsibility.

During his teenage years, Jack would have yanked the letter out and read it in a heartbeat. And because he'd honed some skills he wasn't particularly proud of, he'd have been able to return it to its former position so no one would ever suspect a thing. But that was before he met Alex, Maddie's late husband, and that brought him to his current dilemma.

Take care of her, Jack. Promise me.

Jack didn't like making promises. If he didn't make them, he didn't have to worry about keeping them. But how did you turn down a dying man? So he'd made the damn promise and spent the last year making good on it by inviting his friend's widow to dinner once a month and calling her at least once in between. He'd have preferred dining at a noisy, impersonal restaurant in downtown Atlanta, but Maddie insisted on inviting him to her house for a home-cooked meal.

So far, Maddie hadn't required much caretaking. The woman had a good job and she'd inherited her husband's estate, which hadn't placed her on the *Forbes* list, but she was in the "quite financially comfortable" category.

He bent down a corner of the letter and tilted his head. Maybe just a peek.

"Jack, did you find it?" a female voice asked from behind him.

Busted.

Oh yeah. He'd come into the kitchen to find Parmesan cheese.

He waved the container in her direction and pulled the phone from its cradle. "I need to check my voice mail." He tucked the receiver under his chin and punched out the numbers.

"I'll start soaking these pots while you do."

Efficient Maddie. The multi-tasking queen. So much for getting a further look at the letter. Jack made a show of listening to his messages and hung up.

"Ready?" Maddie dried her hands and carefully folded the towel.

"After you." Jack motioned toward the cozy dining room and followed her. He glanced over his shoulder one last time at the paper, which still screamed *Read Me*.

Later, if he was lucky.

Even after years of client dinners at expensive eateries, dining with real dishes, matching silverware and cloth napkins made Jack uncomfortable. But every month Maddie prepared a feast fit for a king and served it to him as if he were royalty.

He liked her well enough. Hell, he liked her too well. Who wouldn't? She was gorgeous and brilliant, tall and curvy with legs designed to wrap around a man's waist. When it wasn't styled and hair-sprayed into place, her chestnut-colored hair dipped across her forehead and sometimes partially obscured one eye. The ends curled slightly where they brushed her shoulders. And her eyes. They were the color of rich brandy dotted with flecks of gold and ringed with long, thick lashes. A man could imagine staring into them as he drove her over the edge.

Ain't gonna happen, buster.

No, Jack would never experience her legs wrapped around him, see her dark hair against his pillow or melt in the depths of her eyes because that wasn't why they had dinner every month. Even though he found his late business partner's wife unbelievably attractive, he wouldn't act on the attraction. He couldn't.

Make her keep living, Jack. Help her find a good man.

He often regretted the promise, not because he minded looking in on Madelyn Prescott; to the contrary, he enjoyed it and he shouldn't. But, more to the point, no one should have to depend on him for anything.

In Jack's experience, promises were as fragile as soap bubbles. One good puff of air would send them elsewhere and they could be crushed with two fingers.

Yeah, he liked Maddie, and if they'd met under different circumstances, she probably would have spent some time tangled in his sheets. Or he'd have died giving the pursuit his all. Now all he could do was sit awkwardly across a table from the gorgeous but untouchable woman.

Hell, if it weren't for Alex, Jack would probably be eating corn dogs and cabbage in a prison somewhere instead of enjoying a hot meal with the man's widow.

If nothing else Jack could make sure she didn't do anything dumb like buy stock in some wildly speculative venture or cash in her 401(k) and invest it in a pyramid scheme.

"Butter?"

The question pulled him from his thoughts, and he glanced at the plate Maddie thrust toward him.

He could juggle a hammer and a mouthful of nails, sling a square of shingles over his shoulder and climb up a ladder with ease. But put him at a fancy dinner table and he suddenly grew ten thumbs.

"Uh, sure thanks."

Jack carved off a chunk and slathered it on the hot roll perched on the edge of his plate. Then he forked spaghetti into his mouth, fighting the urge to suck the long strands like he'd done as a kid when Chef Boyardee had been a regular feature on the menu.

The clink of forks against china plates was all that broke the silence. And it was driving Jack mad.

"Did the lawyers call you about the paperwork to finalize the probate?"

Jack nodded around a mouthful of buttered roll and swallowed. "I don't know why you hired that big firm to handle Alex's will. I'd have been perfectly satisfied to let you do it, Maddie."

"I'm a family lawyer, Jack," she explained, carefully wiping a spot of sauce from her bottom lip. "I'm more comfortable having an experienced probate attorney handle this."

Wonder what it would be like to kiss that sauce off her lip? Aw, hell. He'd been too long without a woman in his bed, and now he was fantasizing about the one woman in the world who was completely off limits.

"But Alex *is* family," he replied, reeling his thoughts back to the conversation at hand. "Was family."

"And I want to make sure the will is probated properly. I couldn't bear the thought of you losing the business if I screwed something up."

Screw something up? Not Maddie. Screwing up was Jack's domain. Or at least it had been until Alex got sick and Jack had to step up to the plate and run Prescott-Worth.

"And what about you? Are you making sure you're taken care of, too?"

"I don't need to be taken care of." Maddie stabbed a piece of lettuce with her fork.

Alex thought you did.

"As far as the estate goes, the business is yours, and Alex funded an endowment at Tech. He had his broker set up a good retirement fund for Mildred, too," she continued, glancing around the professionally decorated room. "And the rest is mine."

Mildred Thomas managed the Prescott-Worth office, and the woman had been with Alex since he'd started his first construction firm twenty years ago, fresh out of Georgia Tech with a degree in building construction.

"I keep trying to convince Millie to go ahead and retire, but she just looks at me with those big blue eyes and asks how I'd manage without her." Jack's mouth twitched with amusement.

"She's not old enough to retire, even if she wanted to. And you know she hates being called Millie."

"She's sixty, and if you tell her I told you her age, I'll buy her a dozen roses and a pound of Godiva chocolates every day to convince her you're lying. Contrary to popular opinion, retirement isn't about age; it's about money. And thanks to Alex, she has plenty of it if she wants to retire tomorrow or in five years." Jack waggled his eyebrows mischievously. "What's more, she tells me every day how special I am. You wouldn't want to ruin me in her eyes, would you?"

Maddie tried to suppress a laugh. "You're special all right. A special pain in the—"

"Now, now. Is that any way to treat a guest?" Jack leaned back in his chair and sipped from his glass of cabernet. "Be careful or I'll tell *Mildred* you're picking on me."

"Like she'd care. Alex was always her favorite..." Her voice trailed off and she glanced around the room again, looking everywhere but Jack's face.

He watched a single tear slide down her cheek and fought the urge to rush around the table and comfort her. To hold her close to him and let her cry on his shoulder. That would be taking care of her, wouldn't it?

Instead, Jack played it safe and changed the subject. "This is very good, by the way," he said, pointing at his plate of pasta with the fork. "But I'd have been happy to take you out for spaghetti so you wouldn't have had to rush home from work and cook."

"I miss him so much," she whispered. "He was all I had, and we thought we had a wonderful future together. But it doesn't always work that way, does it? We don't all get a happy ending to our love stories."

Jack shook his head, afraid if he said anything his voice would crack and he'd surrender to the tightness that banded his heart. He was more afraid, however, that if he gave in to it, he might never recover.

* * *

Maddie cautiously observed the man sitting across from her. He'd been her husband's best friend and business partner, and in the year since Alex died, he'd been her once-a-month dinner companion. She'd tried to put him off; she'd made every excuse in the book, but

Jack was stubborn. At least she'd been able to convince him to have their dinners at her house where she held the home turf advantage.

They engaged in awkward small talk and fumbled around the fact they'd lost someone dear to them. Maddie probably knew more about Jack than he was aware of.

At the end of his life, Alex had been full of painkillers that sometimes loosened his tongue. They'd talked about the good times and bad, and their dreams for the future—a future that died with Alex.

And Alex had confessed something the night before he died.

I missed it, Maddie. Kids, car pools, Little League, AARP. All of it. I thought I could have it all. That we could have it all. Guess I was wrong. Don't make the same mistake. Please. Promise me you won't let life pass you by.

She'd agreed, but the promise was laughable really. At thirty-three she was way too young for AARP.

They'd wanted children. They'd celebrated their fourth wedding anniversary just before Alex had been diagnosed with lymphoma. Maddie had often wished they had thought to preserve Alex's sperm before he started chemotherapy. Even if he had survived, more than likely he'd have been sterile. Had she thought of it, she could have used Alex's sperm and not needed a donor.

Lately, Alex's words had run through her mind with increasing frequency. Two months ago she had made a decision. She wasn't necessarily hearing her biological clock ticking more loudly, but the desire for a child had been steadily growing stronger. She found herself stopping to stare through the window of the baby shop at the mall and any time she heard a baby's laughter, she couldn't help but smile.

The idea had come inadvertently from one of her professional colleagues who had done legal work for a local sperm bank and fertility clinic. Maddie had logged onto their website and browsed through the donor files until she found him.

Donor number 1580. Stature and coloring similar to Alex. High IQ, athletic, no known genetic problems. A pediatric physician who donated sperm to give others the opportunity to enjoy parenthood.

Too bad her own parents hadn't enjoyed the experience of parenthood.

She wasn't them. Maddie knew she'd be a good mother. And so what if she didn't have a husband? Being in a loving one-parent home was far better than living in a broken one as she had.

"I miss him, too, Maddie," Jack whispered back. Then he drew in a deep breath and straightened in his chair. "But we have to go on. We have to keep living. It's what Alex wanted us to do."

Jack lifted his wine glass as if to raise a toast.

Maddie pulled a tissue from her pocket and swiped at her eyes. Lifting her glass of water as well, she pasted a smile on her face.

"It's time to move on, Jack," she told him. "And I think it's time we stopped these monthly pity parties. We struggle to carry on polite conversation. I choke on every bite of food. You sit there feeling sorry for me. I've made some decisions in the last few weeks that will move my life in a new direction. I only hope you're able to do the same."

"Is that what the sperm canister is all about?"

Water spewed everywhere.

"How…" Her cheeks burned from embarrassment.

"The letter behind your phone. You aren't seriously considering going to a sperm bank, are you?"

Maddie pushed away from the table and picked up her plate, heading toward the kitchen. "And if I am, what makes it your business?" Chagrin replaced the previous awkwardness.

Jack followed, juggling his plate in one hand as he nudged open the door to the kitchen with his elbow.

"What the hell are you thinking? You're going to get yourself knocked up by some total stranger so you can play Mommy?" He took her plate and scraped it into the sink.

"No one is *knocking me up*, as you so charmingly put it." She crossed her arms and leaned against the counter. "The procedure is done in an office by a doctor and—"

"I know how the hell it's done."

"Oh? I wasn't aware The Playboy Channel televised medical documentaries."

"I watch The Learning Channel, too. Surprised?" He loaded the dishwasher while she looked on in amazement. "What? I'm housebroken. I'm not Emeril, but I cook a mean meatloaf and mashed potatoes." He squirted dish gel in the dispenser. "From scratch," he added.

"Quite honestly, nothing about you would surprise me, Jack. What did surprise me was my husband being in business with you. You were as different as…as…"

"Champagne and beer?" he suggested as he rinsed the sink. "Caviar and hot dogs? You and me?"

"You got that right." Maddie lifted her chin defiantly.

"Alex and I may have had different personality types, but we were in complete agreement on the company. We worked hard, ran an honest business and it paid off." He slammed the dishwasher door, then spun and took two steps toward her. "And I intend to continue working hard and keep Prescott-Worth profitable."

"I didn't mean to insinuate—"

"Yes you did, Maddie. You've looked down your nose at me since the first time we met. I didn't grow up in the same kind of neighborhood you did. I didn't go to the same kind of fancy college." He moved toward her and invaded her personal space. "Hell, I didn't even go to college until after I started working for Alex. He encouraged me to go and helped me stick it out."

"You have a degree?" she asked with a mixture of amazement and disbelief. "From where? Earl's School of Hammering and Screwing? No pun intended, of course."

"Of course," he replied with distinct mockery. "And yes, I have a degree from Georgia State. Dean's list every semester."

"I had no idea." She had learned all sorts of new information about Jack Worth tonight.

"I've only stuck around because of that damned promise I made—"

"Promise?" She became defensive. "What promise?"

"It doesn't involve you so just forget about it." A momentary look of uneasiness crossed his face.

"If I've been feeding you for the past year because of it, then it most certainly does involve me."

"I would have taken you to any restaurant in Atlanta. I told you that every month. Let it go, Maddie." He ground out the final words.

"What. Promise?" She edged closer and used the same bulldog approach with Jack she used in the courtroom with a belligerent witness.

Jack opened his mouth then snapped it shut again. She saw the moment of capitulation in his expressive blue eyes.

"He made me promise I'd look after you. That I'd make sure you didn't do anything crazy or crawl in a hole somewhere and withdraw from the world." He hesitated, and when he looked down toward the floor she knew there was more.

"And?"

His gaze met hers and became steely, and she could see the muscles in his jaw working. "And that I'd protect you," he finished.

She and Jack stood almost nose to nose. She could smell his spicy aftershave, feel his breath against her face. His pupils were dilated, and she was certain if she'd placed her fingers against his throat, his pulse would pound against them.

Her own heart raced as it always did when she'd successfully cross-examined a witness or protected the rights of children whose parents tried to place them in the crosshairs of their divorce.

She also felt a flutter in her belly that shouldn't be there. It morphed into a flicker and threatened to become a flame before she tamped it back down. This wasn't the way a woman felt toward a man she didn't care about. This was the way Alex had made her feel. Perhaps her traitorous body had just been without a man for so long it had lost any sense of good judgment.

"Are you happy now?" Jack shoved his hands deep in his pockets and his blue gaze never wavered.

Maddie's throat tightened as she digested this last bit of information. "So that's what the supper club has been about? Taking care of poor Maddie?"

Jack pursed his lips and nodded almost imperceptibly.

"Well Maddie can take care of herself. I've been doing it for years and managing just fine. So consider your obligation fulfilled. As of now, next month's dinner party has been cancelled."

Chin raised a notch, spine straight, Maddie turned on her heel and moved back toward the dining room. "When you've finished with kitchen duty, you can let yourself out." She couldn't contain the haughty tone. How *dare* they think she couldn't manage on her own! She directed her anger as much at her late husband as toward his misguided friend.

"Taking care of yourself?" Jack asked, stopping her. "You have a canister of sperm on the way. Hell, maybe it's already in the freezer, sitting there between the mint chocolate chip and last night's leftover chicken casserole." Jack strode to the refrigerator and yanked open the freezer door.

"It isn't there. It isn't even here. Apparently you didn't snoop enough to see that the letter is just a reply to my inquiry." Irritation laced her voice.

A sigh of relief hissed between his lips and he rubbed the back of his neck. "Thank God."

"Well thank you for the vote of confidence, but don't relax just yet. I have a shipment arriving next month."

"Don't do it, Maddie. How do you know the guy's not a serial killer or a bank robber or a…a…"

"A womanizing, beer-swilling, Playboy Channel-watching construction business owner?" Maddie's left eyebrow rose a fraction of an inch.

"In the flesh, babe," he announced. He spread his arms wide, which pulled his polo shirt tight across his broad chest and emphasized the width of his shoulders.

"Not that I owe you any sort of explanation, but they do have certain safeguards in place so that my baby won't be fathered by a serial killer."

"What kind of safeguards? Not that you owe me any sort of explanation or anything," he said, his sarcasm evident as he threw her words back at her.

Maddie hesitated, contemplating whether to ignore the question, since she didn't need to explain her actions, or to answer his questions to satisfy his curiosity and get him off her case. The latter won out.

"The clinic has questionnaires and tests for potential donors. Evaluations. Background checks."

"I suppose they have a mail-order catalog with these guys listed in alphabetical order?" Jack's gaze shifted toward a pile of mail on the granite countertop under the phone.

Maddie huffed out an impatient breath. "It's online and you search by physical characteristics, ethnic background, that sort of thing."

"And then these men are paid to sit in a recliner and watch porn? Sounds to me like they're making money hand over fist." Jack winked in her direction. "Pun intended."

Maddie rolled her eyes. "You make it sound like something perverted. It's much more clinical than that."

"Clinical? How the hell's a guy supposed to get off if it's all stainless steel and bright lights?"

Maddie clenched her fists and fought the urge to strangle him. Arguing with Jack was like arguing with a brick wall.

"It's not *that* clinical. But it's not the back room at The Cheetah Club either. I doubt *you* could pass muster at the sperm bank."

Jack clutched his chest and staggered backward. "I'm wounded, Maddie. How do you know about The Cheetah Club anyway?"

Great work, Maddie. Nothing like the mention of a gentlemen's club and topless bar to take Jack's mind straight to the gutter.

Then a slow, sexy grin spread across his face. "Maybe I should give it a try. The sperm bank, that is, since I've already been to the other."

She had no doubt he was a regular customer, but was he suggesting...?

"You're out of your mind. There's no way."

"Why not?" His tone contained a hint of challenge.

Why not? A couple dozen reasons came to mind along with a brief vision of his muscular body atop hers, and a powerful current zinged from her brain and settled in her belly, just below where the previous flutter had been. Or maybe she'd just put too much garlic in the sauce because she'd have to be a raving lunatic to consider Jack Worth as a potential sperm donor.

"Give me one good reason why not. I have a higher than average IQ and I'm incredibly handsome."

"Humble, too."

"I'm in good physical shape and my blood tests are clean. You know me, Maddie. You wouldn't have to worry about any unknown factors."

"That's precisely why it's a bad idea, Jack. I know you." God, did she know him. She'd heard some stories about his exploits, and while Alex never said anything, Millie had let a few remarks slip. In addition there were a couple of times around town she and Alex had run into Jack to find him with a drink in one hand and some busty blonde clinging to him like flypaper.

"Look, Maddie. I promised Alex I'd look after you, and if you're determined to go through with this damn crazy stunt, at least let me be the donor."

Two

Jack leaned back in his desk chair and pinched the bridge of his nose in an attempt to ward off an impending headache. Lack of sleep had him in a foul mood. He could smell the coffee brewing, and he was tempted to sneak a cup before it finished. It would no doubt taste like sludge, but it would kick-start his system with caffeine. Hell, he knew it would taste bad anyway since he'd tried to stretch the last few scoops of coffee, but desperate times called for recycled coffee grounds.

Somewhere between eating a spaghetti dinner and saying good-bye, Jack had offered to become a sperm donor. Who opened his mouth last night and put words into it? From the look on Maddie's face you'd have thought he'd volunteered to sleep with her instead of stepping into an exam room to watch *Debbie Does Dallas* with a paper cup in one hand.

He'd let himself out after rendering Maddie speechless. It wasn't easy to leave her dumbstruck, and he'd rather enjoyed watching her stand there with her mouth opening and closing like a fish on dry land.

Of course, he too had reacted to his sudden and uncharacteristic offer. His nightly dreams had alternated between scenes of Dr. Frankenstein in his laboratory, a giant turkey baster and quadruplets that all looked like him and cried incessantly.

But the worst dream was the one of Maddie, her belly enlarged with his baby growing inside, her breasts full and heavy and her face glowing because she was finally going to have the child she wanted.

Satisfaction over keeping his promise warred with guilt over his attraction to her. And if he were honest with himself, he'd have to admit to an attraction that pre-dated last night.

What in the hell had he been thinking? He had let his guilt and his gonads rule. The little head below his belt had short-circuited the one atop his shoulders.

His computer completed the boot-up process and he logged onto the Internet. He typed in the URL for the Metropolitan Atlanta Cryobank Services website because he wanted to see just what he might have gotten himself into.

He scanned the donor listings first, and oh God, had Maddie been wrong. He could easily pass muster here. Or at least he thought he could. Next he clicked over to the donor requirements page and delved into the details of sperm washing and cryopreservation.

Why hadn't Alex banked his own sperm if he knew he was dying? Curious as he was, Jack wouldn't be so presumptuous as to ask Maddie such a personal question. Lord knows, though, if she accepted his offer, he'd be answering a panel of much more personal questions at MACS.

Maybe questions like, "Would you like us to preserve your sperm, Mr. Worth, just in case the unforeseeable happens and your sperm production ceases?" Jack felt his groin tighten at the thought of unforeseeable interruption of his sperm production.

Easy, boys. You're okay.

Of course, that's what Alex had probably thought, too, before cancer swooped in at age forty-two and his life had gone to hell. So why hadn't Alex made a deposit with one of the friendly tellers at the sperm bank? Jack thought back to the day Alex had dropped the bombshell of his lymphoma diagnosis. Apparently he'd been sick for a while before he let anyone know. Maybe he simply hadn't had time to bank sperm—or even consider it—before chemotherapy had rendered him unable to do much more than sleep in his La-Z-Boy between bouts of puking.

Lost in more biological subject matter than he'd faced since his first year of college, he failed to notice his office manager's arrival until she stood beside him with a mug of coffee in each hand.

"I stopped by the coffee shop on my way in and picked up a couple bags of your favorite poison. I dumped that muck you made and fixed another pot, and please tell me the Leverniers didn't cancel the contract for their mini-mansion and you're looking for other ways to make money." She nodded at his computer screen as she set a cup of steaming fragrant brew beside his keyboard, then she lowered herself into the leather chair in the corner of the small office. "And if you expect me to turn tricks on Peachtree Street to boost revenue, you're about forty years too late, honey."

A gulp of coffee scalded its way to his stomach before he saw her wink and a devilish grin curved her lips.

"Aw hell, Millie. You might be over fifty, but you still turn heads. You turn mine every day."

"Yeah," she quipped. "Round and round like that little girl in the horror movie." The plump older woman pushed aside a blueprint tube on the chair-side table and set down her coffee mug.

"I've caught you in some pretty compromising situations, Jack Worth, but this one has even me puzzled. And don't think I didn't catch that decade you shaved off my age. Empty flattery will get you nowhere with me." She pointed toward the computer screen, filled with images of spermatozoa and smiling babies. "I know this business is as solid as the gold in Fort Knox. If you were looking at some other kind of clinic, I might have figured you dipped your wick in the wrong place and you were trying to deal with the aftermath."

Jack tried not to squirm in his chair under the woman's steely grey-eyed scrutiny. She'd been with the company since the day Alex started it, and in the early days she'd worked for little more than minimum wage to help insure its success. She'd also listened to her share of sob stories and crazy excuses from him and played nursemaid through any number of rotten hangovers.

"But for the life of me I can't figure out why you're looking into a sperm bank. Unless..." Her normally rosy complexion paled. "You're not...? Like Alex?"

"No! Oh, no. I'm healthy as a horse." He minimized the screen and debated telling Millie about his offer. Alex had mentored him after his one big brush with the law, and Millie had mothered him after his own mother had run off to the Florida Gulf coast with her latest man du jour. Now, Jack was co-owner of Prescott-Worth. No, make that sole owner of a highly successful residential construction business. P-W built homes for NFL quarterbacks and Major League Baseball pitchers and cable television network executives. So why did he feel like a schoolboy caught playing spin the bottle with the cutest girl in class?

Maybe because he'd been caught playing "donate the sperm" with the boss's widow. But maybe he hadn't been caught because Millie admitted the website puzzled her.

"Well, if you're not trying to bank your sperm before you die then—"

"It's just curiosity, okay? I saw something on one of the cable television stations last night and I just wanted to check it out. Don't you have the mid-month reports to do or something?"

"Or something, yeah." Millie pushed herself up from the chair and grabbed her coffee mug. "Whatever you say, boss. Mid-month reports coming right up, even if it is only the first." She paused in the doorway separating Jack's small office from the reception area and shot him a pointed look. "Just don't think about me while you're in that little room with a dirty magazine."

Jack heard her laughing as he maximized the screen and stared at the images of happy couples, tiny babies and medical instruments necessary for artificial insemination. His part was easy—enjoyable actually. Maddie was the one who'd be subjected to God knows what.

Mentally he superimposed Maddie's face onto the screen. She was going to get pregnant one way or another. He'd promised to look out for her, though he doubted Alex had anything like this in mind when he made his dying request. Hell, the man would probably roll over in his grave at the very idea of Jack helping Maddie get pregnant. Thank goodness he hadn't offered to do it the old-fashioned way.

Jack clicked back to the donor page and compared himself to the men listed. Oh yeah, he'd definitely pass muster. But there'd be no cryo-tank in the storage freezer with Jack's name on it. No sperm-sicles in his future. He'd take his chances with the unforeseeable.

Now he just had to convince Maddie that this was the best route to take. The money she'd save by not buying donor sperm would start a nice college fund for her child. He'd give her a day or two and then follow up.

Closing the MACS website, he gulped the rest of his coffee and pushed away from his desk.

"Millie? Would you pull the Levernier file for me? And is there more coffee?" He needed to focus on business now so his statement to Maddie would be true. He intended for Prescott-Worth to maintain the same level of respect it had always enjoyed. He'd prove to Maddie—and everyone else—that he wasn't the screw-up he'd once been. He'd keep his promise and prove that Alex's trust in him wasn't misplaced—that is if he could get rid of the niggling memory of a child growing up without a father.

* * *

Maddie closed the folder in front of her and conceded defeat. She'd been staring at the particulars of the Freeman case for two hours and aside from consuming two cups of tea and a chocolate candy bar, she'd made no other progress.

If you're determined to go through with this damn crazy stunt, at least let me be the donor.

Jack's words from the previous evening still played through her mind. She shouldn't let anything Jack Worth said bother her, and normally she wouldn't. But he and Alex had conspired behind her back to treat her like some sort of helpless, grief-stricken weakling unable to control her own life.

Maddie was more than capable of controlling her life, despite being the product of her parents' Wimbledon version of child custody, with Maddie lobbed back and forth so often even the spectators were left confused. Alex had understood and always made sure she had choices in everything that concerned her life. Now Jack was calling her choice a damn crazy stunt and trying to insinuate himself into the situation.

Why not? He was a serial womanizer who was all about short-term, temporary, limited-engagement relationships. When the title changed on the local movie theater marquee, so did the woman in Jack's life.

Maddie, on the other hand, was the kind of woman who dreamed of balancing home and hearth, white picket fences and a meaningful career. Unfortunately her dreams had been shattered before she and Alex had been able to begin to realize them.

But maybe short-term and temporary wasn't so bad after all. At the most basic level, Jack had admirable qualities and a solid work ethic. She had seen that up close during the final months of Alex's illness. And as much as it pained her, the newly discovered knowledge of his dean's list academic achievements impressed her. She couldn't even put that on her own résumé.

As long as he posed no health threat—and the clinic would check him from the top of his head to the soles of his feet—perhaps Jack wasn't such a bad choice after all.

She wasn't going to *sleep* with him. All she needed was his bodily fluids. He'd donate at the clinic and her doctor would inseminate her in his office. End of story. If Jack made multiple donations, she should have plenty of samples in case she needed several attempts to get pregnant.

"Are you finished with the Freeman file?"

Maddie looked up and saw Tess Callahan leaning against the doorframe. She and Tess had joined the firm at the same time nearly a decade ago, and as newcomers to both the firm and to Atlanta, they had bonded immediately.

"Uhm, no, but if you need it right now, go ahead and take it. I can work on it later." Maddie held out the folder and hoped her friend didn't pick up on her dour mood.

Tess stepped to the desk and accepted the papers. "What's troubling you, Mads? And don't bother trying to lie because I can see right through you. Something's bugging you and those bags under your eyes would cost you extra on any commercial airline."

Maddie reflexively glanced to her right and caught her reflection in the mirrored back of a bookshelf. If sleep continued to elude her, she'd have to pay more attention to her makeup—dab a little more concealer under her eyes, brush a little more blush on her cheeks—because the last thing she needed was for anyone at work to become suspicious. Once everything was finalized, once she was pregnant, then she'd break the news.

"It's nothing really." *Except possibly a pregnancy.* "The final probate on Alex's will is going through and there's been a lot of paperwork. A lot of memories."

"You know I'll help you with anything you need. All you have to do is ask."

"I know. I thought it was better to let another firm handle it so there'd be no questions about impartiality."

Tess nodded knowingly. "If you need to get away from things, we can go to the Sun Dial tonight and leave the rest of the world at our feet."

The revolving restaurant sat atop the Westin Peachtree hotel and looked down on the city. It just might be the perfect place to forget wills, estates and sperm offers. But not tonight.

"Maybe next week?"

"Sure thing. You just name the day." Tess walked away, then stopped in the doorway and looked back over her shoulder. "Promise you'll call if you need to talk, okay?"

Maddie made a crossing motion over her heart and smiled as Tess left the office. Once she'd decided one way or another about a donor, she had no doubt she and Tess would burn up the phone lines talking it over. But in the meantime, Maddie had to entertain Jack's offer.

If she knew anything at all about Jack Worth, it was that he wouldn't forget what he'd suggested and would probably call soon for her answer. Maybe not tonight since only twenty-four hours had passed. But he would call and she needed to have an answer ready for him. A well-thought-out answer complete with logical reasons to support her decision.

She opened the word processor on her computer, and then closed it almost as soon as it filled the screen. While the firm wasn't known for snooping into its employees' computer files, she couldn't take a chance on her plan getting out just yet.

Pulling a new yellow legal pad from her desk drawer, drew a line down the middle of the page and labeled the left side <u>CON</u> and the right <u>PRO</u>.

On both sides she wrote *friend of the family*. The fact he was Alex's friend and business partner meant Maddie knew a lot about Jack—or could find out either from Millie or through the private investigator she used for some of her cases.

She knew a lot about him, but certainly not everything. Jack most likely wouldn't appreciate being investigated, but what he didn't know wouldn't hurt him. This was her child, after all, and a man's background mattered.

If he'd been any of the candidates whose files she'd perused on the MACS website, he'd have been investigated to the roots of his teeth. She'd know his whole life history as well as how many teeth he had, how many were real or crowned and if he'd ever had orthodontic work.

His being Alex's business partner—and new owner of the business—meant some people might question her decision if she agreed to Jack's offer. Of course, who said she had to name the donor? She wouldn't know the name of a MACS donor, so anonymity wasn't out of the ordinary.

Next she wrote *Free* on the PRO side and *MACS Expense* on the other. While she wasn't lacking for money, Maddie wasn't a spendthrift. She'd gladly pay the going rate for the right sperm, but every website she'd consulted said conception rates from artificial insemination were much lower than from the old-fashioned way. If it took more than a couple attempts, she could make a serious dent in her savings account. With Jack, there would be no expense. At least not a monetary one.

But what if the child looked exactly like Jack? She added *possibility of strong resemblance* to the CON list. On the PRO side, she wrote *attractive* and *healthy*.

Jack had donated blood religiously every eight weeks for Alex, and good health was a requirement for blood donors, especially when the recipient was a chemo patient. She knew Jack had a reputation as a serial dater, but if he had any diseases, he'd have been turned away at the blood bank.

Yet, Alex had been dead for a year—plenty of time for Jack to catch something—so Maddie added *dating habits* to the CON list.

Just before the end, while on a morphine pump, Alex had told her he'd met Jack when the drunken teenager had trashed a construction site. Jack had worked off the damage and had apparently impressed Alex enough to hire him and then later make him a partner. *Past brush with the law* went onto the CON side while *Alex trusted him* balanced it on the other. Even though Jack wouldn't be involved in her child's life, personality and character traits were important and must be considered.

With MACS, she wouldn't know much about the donor's character and personality. Was he donating for altruistic reasons or just for the money? Donor 1580 had appeared to be of good character based on his profile, but ever since Jack had raised the issue of serial killers and bank robbers…

She shook off the negative thought. Jack's behavior during Alex's illness—taking over running the business, the blood donations, the constant visits—showed he cared. Really cared. And, she had to admit, it meant something to both she and Alex; Jack had been a comfort and dependable.

Lastly, she added the two most important factors in her decision: *Custody waiver* versus *possible custody battle*. Even though she'd insist on an agreement to absolve Jack of any parental responsibility, the possibility he'd sue for visitation and custody could not be discounted. While Jack didn't impress her as the family type, who knew what changes could occur in the future? She'd have to take

Jack at his word since legally he couldn't sign away any responsibility for a child. Those rights belonged to the child, not the birth parent. After being bounced between her parents for years, she wanted to avoid that fate for her baby if at all possible.

Maddie knew she'd come under fire from some people for her decision to have a child as a single parent. But to her way of thinking it was better to live in a loving single-parent home than be in a home with feuding parents who used a child as a pawn.

Confident she'd covered every contingency, she ripped the sheet off the legal pad, slid it inside an old manila folder and slipped the folder into her briefcase. She'd study it later at home over a cup of tea. Or perhaps a glass of wine. After a restless night and the brutal day of drowsiness that had followed, Maddie needed something to help her slide into a deep, restorative sleep.

* * *

Three nights later, Maddie unwrapped a towel from her head and draped it across the side of the tub. After pulling on jeans and a t-shirt, she finger-combed her still damp hair, then padded to the kitchen in her bare feet. She grabbed a soda from the refrigerator and while opening it, spotted the letter from the sperm bank.

Why hadn't she filed it away with the other information from MACS? She was usually organized to a fault, and this one slip had resulted in major consequences. Once she had learned about Jack's deal with Alex, she put a stop to his checking on her. But, would using him as a donor be like jumping out of the frying pan and into the fire?

She tugged the paper from behind the telephone where it had remained since she had received it. Sliding into a chair at her kitchen table, she smoothed the folded sheets of paper and laid them beside the dog-eared folder, opened to display her list.

Jack would be arriving soon and she'd promised him an answer. Maybe she should call and postpone their meeting. That would calm the heavy sensation of dread in her belly. But it wouldn't change the overall picture. Mentally reviewing the list she could now recite from memory, Maddie assessed the pros and cons once more before closing the folder.

Jack was a known quantity. He'd told her he was "clean," and despite his brush with the law at eighteen, she knew him to be a basically good person. Jack had taken over all of the business when Alex was too sick to work and never once grumbled, even when he had to work over eighty hours a week to get it all done.

Also, Jack was tall with dark coloring and was, admittedly, handsome. Together they'd make a beautiful baby.

Don't go there. Maddie gave herself a mental reprimand and thanked the doctor who'd figured out that artificial insemination methods used on dairy cattle would also work with humans. Otherwise she'd have to crawl in bed with Jack and, oh God, but that created a vision of him lying between rumpled sheets and looking like a magazine's "Sexiest Man Alive." She did not need another complication to what was already going to be quite a sticky situation. Maddie needed to view Jack only as a vial of donor sperm and not as a man.

Maddie shoved the image from her mind and focused on the impending task. She'd made her decision, right or wrong, and the time to announce it was at hand. In any case, she and Jack needed to stop their dinners and move on. With Jack running Prescott-Worth by himself and her likely dealing with pregnancy and preparing a nursery for a baby, neither would have time.

A soft rap sounded at the back door. Through the glass panel she could see Jack standing on the other side. She motioned for him to enter, then placed the letter in the folder and closed it. She could still postpone her announcement, but it wouldn't do anything except to drag out the inevitable.

He opened the door and began to step into the kitchen, then toed off his muddy boots and nudged them aside on the back deck. He still wore clothes from working on site—a faded Braves t-shirt, well-worn jeans that hugged him like a second skin and white socks permanently stained from Georgia red clay.

"Would you like coffee or something to eat?" *Maybe a hot shower with an audience?*

"I've eaten. I stopped at The Varsity for a couple hot dogs. I should have called and asked if you wanted one. The coffee sounds good though."

When Maddie started to rise, he held out his hand toward her. "I can get it. Just stay where you are."

With a familiarity that should have rung warning bells in her head, Jack opened one cabinet to retrieve a mug, a drawer to get a spoon and then pulled a carton of half-and-half from the refrigerator and added a dollop to his mug before filling it. "Want some, too?" he asked, holding up the mug.

"I've already had my caffeine limit for the day. But thanks."

Jack moved back to the table and sat, blowing on the liquid before taking a long drink.

"So you've made your decision?" He raised one eyebrow and stared at her. "You could have told me over the phone."

"I thought something this important needed to be handled in person. I know you're tired and I won't keep you long." Maddie knew Jack had a thirty-minute drive home to his loft just outside the perimeter.

"So what do you say, Maddie? Is it going to be me or the Boston Strangler?"

"Since you put it that way," she replied, her throat tight from irritation. Couldn't Jack ever take anything seriously? Maybe she'd made the wrong decision after all.

He set the cup down, laid his palms flat on the table and leaned forward. "I'm sorry. Really. Can I have a do-over?"

Maddie studied his face, searching for something to convince her he was sincere. She saw the muscles relax around his eyes and his gaze never wavered from hers, and she took it as a sign. Jack usually had the attention span of a gnat, and the fact he'd never once glanced toward the folder on the table or looked to see if the letter was still wedged behind the phone encouraged her.

"Go ahead," she said.

Jack sat up straighter and released a long breath. Was that worry in his eyes? Was he actually concerned she might tell him no? Or perhaps it was relief that he wouldn't have to follow through on an impulsive offer.

"I can only imagine how difficult this must be for you and I apologize for acting like a jackass. Whatever your decision, I'll support you in any way I can."

"Thank you. I appreciate that." Maddie thumbed the edge of the folder briefly before continuing. "I made a list of all the reasons it was a good idea to let you be the donor and a list of all the reasons it was a bad idea—"

"And after you made your list and checked it twice, you decided I was naughty and not nice?"

Maddie closed her eyes and took a cleansing breath before opening them again.

"I'm doing it again, huh?"

She hesitated and then nodded.

"Are you going to let me see the list?" he asked, eyeing the folder for the first time.

She closed her eyes again and her shoulders slumped.

"I take it that's a no. And I'm also guessing I didn't make the cut and you're going with a donor from the clinic." He lifted the mug to his mouth and drained it. "I understand, Maddie. If I was in your position, I probably wouldn't choose me either."

She stared at him in astonishment. How could a man who oozed confidence back away so easily from what had essentially been a challenge? He had all but dared her to use him as a donor and now, without hearing a word of her decision-making process, he had folded his cards and walked away from the table. She had learned a lot about Jack over the last dinner, and this move revealed even more. Maybe the swagger was an act to cover the real Jack—the Jack he didn't want the world to see. A Jack who actually cared for other people.

He rose and walked to the sink, rinsed the mug and set it upside down in the wooden drainer before heading toward the back door. "I'll let myself out. And I've been thinking about our dinners. It's probably time to stop those, too. You're going to be busy with getting pregnant and all that, so you don't need to be worrying about feeding me. I think Alex would be proud of how you've dealt with his death. I know I am."

"I picked you," she stated flatly. "I want you to be my sperm donor."

Up to this point, sperm donation had simply been an abstract medical procedure she had investigated thoroughly. Now it had become real. As concrete as the houses Jack and Alex had built through the years. And while she knew in her gut that choosing Jack instead of Donor 1580 was the right move, it also scared the hell out of her for the same reasons. Donor 1580 was an abstract; Jack was the real deal.

Jack froze with his hand on the doorknob. Slowly he swiveled and faced her once again. "Really? Then forget that part I said about not even picking myself."

Maddie rested her chin on her hand, and a tenuous smile curved her mouth. "It's already forgotten. Go home and sleep on it and see if you change your mind by morning. MACS has a website that should answer any questions you might have."

"I checked it out the other morning at work and nearly sent Millie to an early grave. But there was one question it didn't answer."

"Oh?"

"I just want to know one thing. Does the sperm bank give you a microwave for opening a new account?" Jack's face split into a wide grin as he rushed through the back door.

Oh, damn. He had great genes and damned if he didn't look good *in* jeans, too, but Maddie hoped she hadn't just made the worst decision of her life. She had no designs on Jack, but how might their relationship change once his child was growing inside her? Would her concerns about a custody dispute ever become a reality? She would have to do everything legally possible to ensure that didn't happen—that her decision *was* the right one for her and her baby. Would Jack actually walk away from his child?

Three

"Let me get this straight. You are going to be artificially inseminated and you picked Jack Worth as the donor." Tess's tone made it sound as if Maddie had just announced her resignation, was giving away her house and she'd decided to join a religious cult in the desert of New Mexico.

"Yes," Maddie said, knowing her opinionated friend wasn't through and would not hesitate to let her views be known. "But don't say a word about a possible pregnancy. I don't want anyone here to know yet."

She had ordered lunch for the two of them from the Hawg & Dawg, a nearby hole-in-the-wall barbecue place that combined Atlanta's love of barbecue with the owner's love of Georgia Bulldog football. This way she could reveal her plan to Tess in the privacy of her office and ask for her friend's help with drafting a quasi-legal contract to protect her and her child.

"Oh my God, Maddie, that man is wicked gorgeous." Tess fanned herself in an exaggerated manner. "I was at a party at the Ritz Carlton once and he walked in. He turned women's heads all the way from the door to the bar, and if he swung that way, he could have had the bartender eating out of his hand in ten seconds flat. You'd better watch out because once women find out he's in the sperm donor business, he'll be at the top of the request list, and oh my God, that means he will be making money *hand over fist*."

Maddie sighed. "That's exactly what Jack said. Both of you are sick."

Tess threw back her head and laughed wickedly as Maddie's cheeks flushed with color. "You two are going to make a beautiful baby."

She and Tess were supposed to be drafting a document that would waive Jack's right to custody of any child or children resulting from his sperm donation. He would also waive his financial responsibility since she was fully capable of supporting herself and a baby.

Legally, it represented little more than a handshake on paper; Maddie's only interest was getting pregnant, not setting up housekeeping with Jack.

After Tess's statement, perhaps she should also require that he not donate for anyone but her. She didn't want her child to have half-siblings running all over Atlanta, but for all she knew, that could be the case anyway.

She wondered if any of Jack's romantic conquests had resulted in pregnancy. She'd ask him. This was a business deal, not a love affair. She had a right to know these things, didn't she? Of course, Jack also had a future right to father children if he so desired. Legally, she had no control over his testicles.

"Stick to business," Maddie warned. "We only have an hour to get a good start on this. I have a brief to file this afternoon and need to leave for the courthouse no later than one-fifteen."

"Brief, huh? Do you know if Jack wears briefs or boxers? I've heard that briefs can interfere with good sperm production."

Maddie groaned aloud, aware that her friend was just as prone to veering off subject as Jack had been at her house the night she'd delivered her decision.

"And I wouldn't mind debriefing him at all," Tess said, continuing with the legal humor. "But of course, I'd never step in on your territory. I'll just have to find myself another hunk."

"Jack isn't my *territory*. I don't want anything but his sperm."

"Still, I wouldn't want the father of my baby going out with my best friend, not that I'd ever go out with him anyway. I like my men a little more urbane."

Maddie thought about Tess's statement and wondered why she suddenly felt defensive about Jack. He was courteous and stylish in his own rugged way. "Jack won't really be the baby's *father*. Not in any emotional sense. He'll just provide half the chromosomes and determine whether it's a boy or girl."

"You never did tell me why you decided to use him rather than a sperm bank."

"It's complicated," Maddie said, snagging a potato chip from the bag she and Tess were sharing. "Let's just say the pros outweighed the cons and leave it at that."

"I was just kind of stunned to hear you wanted to have a baby. I know it's none of my business, but—"

"You're right. It isn't any of your business." Maddie shoved her unfinished pork sandwich back in the restaurant bag and tossed it in the wastebasket. Her appetite had disappeared, and what little of the sandwich she'd eaten sat heavily in her stomach. Her baby decision had been a difficult one, and the inclusion of Jack added another layer of complexity. She owed no one an explanation, not even Tess. Especially not Tess, who was as fierce in the courtroom as Maddie was; Maddie didn't want a cross-examination to reveal that she found Jack wicked gorgeous, too.

Tess stiffened and stood, then began gathering the remainder of her lunch and her notes. "We'll finish this later."

"Wait. Don't go. It *is* your business because you're my best friend and you're handling this paperwork for me." Maddie's voice quivered slightly. "Can you forgive me?"

Tess returned to her place across the desk from Maddie.

"Only if you forgive me for opening my big mouth. It's an affliction I struggle with daily."

"It's a deal," Maddie said, chewing on her bottom lip in an attempt to quell the threatening tears. "Alex and I always wanted a family. We had so much love for each other and wanted to share it with a child."

"You don't have to tell me this," Tess insisted.

"Yes, I do. I need you to know why I'm doing this. We'd started talking about kids right before Alex got sick, and then everything happened so fast. Before I could catch my breath he was gone. I looked at the calendar a few months ago and realized he'd been dead almost a year. Then I helped Sylvia Dennis with the work she did for a fertility clinic here and it sparked an idea. So what if most women get a husband first and the baby next? There's no law saying it has to be done in that order. And besides, I have no matrimonial candidates lined up, so I'm going to reverse the process—baby first and then a husband, *if* the right one comes along."

Tess leaned forward in her chair. "You do know you'll get some grief from certain segments of society."

"Yeah, and you'll be right there defending me, won't you?"

"Absolutely, but I refuse to change diapers," she stated emphatically before a glint of amusement flared in her eyes.

Maddie chuckled and then sobered again. "If I do marry again, I want another man like Alex. One who loved me more than life itself, who treated me with respect. One who put my happiness above his own and never—" She stopped abruptly before she gave away too much about her childhood. "Maybe I'll get as lucky a second time, but until I do, I don't want to take chances with my reproductive system. I'm thirty-three, and while that's not old, every year I wait diminishes my chances of pregnancy. So I decided to go ahead and just do it."

"And you're sure Jack is the right man for the job?"

"Positive," she insisted. "If you can work up a rough draft, I can give it to Jack when I see him the day after tomorrow."

"I'll have it for you in forty-eight hours and it'll be as binding as legally possible. You have my word."

* * *

Two days later Maddie's cell phone beeped as she approached her car in the parking lot at Hightower, Leggett and Beck. One of the few non-skyscrapers in downtown Atlanta, the three-story building was dwarfed on all sides. Evan Hightower turned down million-dollar purchase offers weekly in favor of keeping the law firm founded by his grandfather housed in warm and inviting quarters instead of an impersonal and sterile glass and steel tower.

Two blocks from Peachtree Street and less than two miles from the county court house, the office building was also convenient to Maddie's home, something that would be important once there was a baby in the picture. She intended to continue her career, especially her work as an advocate for children. She'd already begun inquiring about nannies so her child could grow up in its own home instead of an institutional day care center.

She pulled her smartphone from her purse and brought it to life. A tap on the screen revealed a voice message from Jack.

Sorry, but I'm running late. I couldn't get a reservation at Bruno's. Call me and we'll figure out another place to meet.

She must have missed his call during her second meeting with Tess, who'd apologized again for opening her big mouth and had then been the bearer of some unsettling information.

She and Jack had planned to meet at an Italian restaurant near her home in the Virginia Highland section of Atlanta. Operating in one of the original commercial "villages" in the area, Bruno's had been a favorite of Alex's and they'd dined there with Jack and Millie several times.

Since she had bad news to deliver to Jack about their arrangement, Maddie had at least wanted to deliver it in familiar surroundings with good food. Top-notch cuisine had a way of softening a blow, though this was more a blow to Maddie than to Jack.

She pressed the call back icon, and he answered after the first ring.

"Where are you?" he asked. "I'm heading in on the 400 and I'm almost to the office. I thought maybe you could meet me at Little Sicily, an Italian place a couple blocks from my office. It's not Bruno's, but it's good. It's across the street from Hooters. If you have trouble finding it, just stop and ask. Everyone knows where Hooters are. Is." Jack laughed at his faux pas. "At least I hope they do."

"I'm not sure Hooters is the best landmark to use." Maddie laughed to cover her annoyance.

"Sure it is. Just ask any guy 'cause he'll know where they are. Anyway, how long do you think it'll take you to get there? I might be able to swing by the office and shower off some of this dirt. We broke ground today on that house I was telling you about last month."

Maddie's annoyance quickly disappeared and was replaced by a vision of Jack standing under a shower, hot water cascading over his neck and shoulders and running down to his—

A soft moan escaped before she could stop it.

"You okay, Maddie?"

"Yeah. Sure," she lied. "My shoulders are just stiff from too much computer work." *Jack. Hot. Stiff.* Not a good thought.

"You'll need to be careful of that once you're pregnant."

Maddie dug her keys out of her purse and mashed the remote to unlock the silver coupe, which had been a fourth anniversary gift from Alex. By their sixth, he was gone.

As she threw her briefcase into the backseat, she realized the automobile wouldn't be very baby-friendly. Getting an infant in and out of a rear-facing car seat in the back of a two-door car would be awkward. She mentally added *new car* to the ever-growing list of changes she'd have to make once a baby entered the picture.

"So how long do you think it will take you to get to the restaurant?" Jack asked.

Maddie realized she'd been wool gathering and calculated the distance, factored in five o'clock traffic and added a little extra time to search for the location. "Forty-five minutes. Maybe a little longer."

"Great. That'll give me time to change. If you get there before me, go ahead and get a table."

* * *

Jack stripped out of his filthy jeans and t-shirt and then hooked his thumbs in the sides of his briefs. Scraping them over his hips and down his legs, he kicked them on the pile of other soiled clothes and stepped into the steaming shower. Construction was dirty work, even for the boss, and he'd never regretted the decision to remodel the Prescott-Worth office space and add a full bathroom.

Now that he was sole owner, he'd thought about putting a futon in what had been Alex's office so he'd have a place to sleep when he'd worked too late and didn't want to drive to his condo.

Sole owner. Who'd ever believe Jack Worth owned his own business? And a legitimate business at that. He'd heard one of his old high school drinking buddies was doing five years in prison for cocaine possession, and another had been killed robbing a convenience store.

During a really stupid period in his life, Jack had vandalized a house being built by one of the good guys. A guy who let him work off the damage, then hired him and eventually let him buy a ten-percent share of the business. When Alex died, Jack had first right of refusal when Maddie decided to sell the business. The pay-off from the life insurance he and Alex had on each other allowed him to buy her out without going into debt. But he would gladly return to being second in command any day to have his friend back working beside him.

After washing the dust from his body and scrubbing his hair and scalp, he rinsed and allowed the hot water to relax his tired muscles. Aware that Maddie was en route to the restaurant, he didn't linger like he usually did. He twisted the faucets, slid open the glass door and pulled a towel from the towel bar. Rubbing it first over his hair, he then ran the thick material over his body until he was dry.

He tossed the towel over the shower door and walked naked to the small vanity against the opposite wall. Wiping away the steam with his hand, he peered into the mirror and used his fingers to brush his hair into place. Satisfied he didn't need to shave, he swished some mouthwash around and then spit it in the sink. He dressed in the clothing he'd worn to the office that morning—khaki pants, black polo shirt and loafers. Wrapping the leather band around his wrist, he fastened his watch and noted he had five minutes to spare before meeting Maddie.

He spotted her at a corner table and worked his way through the Friday night dinner crowd to join her. She wore a jacket made from some material that looked like the upholstery on his grandmother's couch—gray with a flowery design and lapels edged with dark red. The blouse underneath was solid gray and cut low enough for Jack to see where her silver necklace nestled into a hint of cleavage. Her skirt stopped a few inches short of her knee. She had crossed her legs and a black high-heel dangled from the foot that kept time with the music playing over the sound system.

Staring vacantly at the menu and sipping from a glass of red wine, she failed to see Jack approach and jumped slightly when he spoke, spilling a few drops of wine down the front of her blouse.

"I didn't mean to startle you," he said as he grabbed a napkin and reached toward her to dab at the spill. As his hand neared her chest, he reconsidered and pressed the square of starched cotton into her hand.

"Send me your dry-cleaning bill," he urged as he watched her wipe at the stain, sorry he wasn't cleaning it himself. "I hope I didn't keep you waiting long." He needed to change the subject before he embarrassed himself with thoughts of her breasts.

"You didn't," she replied curtly, returning her gaze to the menu and running her finger down the catalog of pasta selections.

Jack studied her lack of facial expression and rigid posture. "Have I said or done something wrong? Are you mad because I asked you to meet me here? Oh wait. It was the Hooter's remark, wasn't it?"

"No, you haven't said or done anything wrong. And I'm not mad about driving here. This is a nice place. I think I'm going to have one of the veal dishes as a matter of fact." She closed the menu and reached for her wine glass.

"So it *was* the Hooter's remark. If I promise to start behaving will you look at me and let me apologize to your face?"

"It wasn't the Hooter's remark. And I'm not mad, so will you just drop it and see if you can get the waiter's attention because I'm starving."

Jack wasn't buying her explanation. Something bugged the hell out of her and he would find out what. But first he'd wine and dine her. Maybe she'd be more cooperative with a full stomach.

He signaled a waiter and placed their orders—veal piccata for her and a rare steak for him. They ate in relative silence, the meal punctuated solely by Jack's periodic comments about the food, the weather, the company's latest project and the bank robbery in broad daylight, which had dominated the TV news for the past week. The masked man in the surveillance videos was probably one of his high school friends.

When they finished their meals and the waiter had removed their plates and replaced them with cups of dark, steaming coffee, Jack decided he'd waited long enough.

"What's going on, Maddie?" he asked as he poured half-and-half into his cup and stirred. "And don't tell me it's nothing. You haven't said a dozen words since you ordered me to *drop it*, and given that we were supposed to talk about the details of our arrangement tonight, I'm wondering if you've changed your mind and just don't want to tell me that I don't need to make my '*bank deposit*.'" Jack used his fingers to make air quotes.

Maddie blinked rapidly and Jack watched as two fat tears escaped and left damp trails down her face. Ah hell, he'd done it again. After his smart-ass performance in her kitchen earlier in the week, he'd vowed to straighten up and stop acting like a jerk. He'd spent the first eighteen years of his life behaving like a juvenile delinquent, and his last stupid stunt had nearly landed him in jail.

He'd spent the years since making up for his actions and proving to everyone he wasn't the same screw-up everyone at his high school had called "Worthless Worth."

That stunt was the reason he had gone to work for Alex Prescott, the reason he'd become Alex's partner and the reason he sat across from the man's crying widow.

"Is that it? You've changed your mind?" He watched one tear reach her chin and fought the urge to reach out and wipe it away. "Aw, honey. It's okay if you want to use an anonymous donor."

Maddie fumbled in her pocket and pulled out a tissue. She dabbed at her cheeks then wadded the tissue in her fist. "It's not that I've changed my mind. I've sort of had it changed for me."

"What do you mean you had it changed for you? This whole baby thing is your choice," he said with quiet emphasis.

Maddie let out a long, audible breath. "Tess called me into her office just before I left work. That's why I missed your call."

"And what does Tess have to do with all this?"

"She was drawing up a contract for me to have you sign—"

"Contract? I didn't think friends had to sign contracts with each other."

"They do when a child is involved. It's nothing major—just something to protect you."

"Why would I need to be protected? We're both going into this deal with all the facts. I visit a closet with a paper cup and a copy of *Hustler*, your doctor does his thing and whammo, you're pregnant. What's to protect?"

"Well, it doesn't really matter now because there won't be paper cups or whammos or anything. The whole thing is off. I appreciate your offer. Really I do, Jack. I know it was awkward for you, and it was really sweet of you to agree to it. And in case you're still thinking about that promise you made to Alex, consider it paid in full."

She reached for her purse and pushed her chair away from the table. "It's getting late and I should be going."

"You still haven't answered my question. What do you mean you had your mind changed for you? What happened?"

Maddie slumped against the back of her chair, a look of defeat playing across her face. "Tess told me Judge Benson, the judge who's been appointing me as *guardian ad litem*, had a heart attack and has been replaced while he recuperates."

"Guardian ad what?"

"*Guardian ad litem*," she explained, twirling the wine glass stem between her thumb and index finger. "When a divorce gets really nasty the court will often appoint an attorney—a *guardian ad litem*—to represent the best interest of the child during the litigation.

With the divorce rate as high as it is, probably a quarter of my caseload is GAL work. It's important to me. Kids don't ask to be put in the middle of divorcing parents and they need an advocate who works solely for them."

"So your judge was replaced. I don't see how this affects our arrangement."

"The new judge is Thomas Jefferson Ward. And yes, that's really his name. I've been before him and he's a misogynistic jerk; he doesn't think women should be lawyers, never mind single pregnant lawyers. Tess told me about Cynthia Hadley, a wonderful attorney, who he dismissed as a GAL last week. No one would be able to prove why he did it, but I can't take the chance he might decide to use me as his next case-in-point."

"But he can't do that, can he? I mean that would be discrimination or a violation of your civil rights or something, wouldn't it?"

"If we were talking about hiring or firing, yes. But GAL appointments fall between the cracks in civil rights law. He can simply choose to not appoint me anymore and there's nothing I can do."

"As much as that sucks, how badly will that affect your income? If you lose that quarter of your work load?" he asked.

"It isn't the money, Jack. It's the work. The children I defend when their parents are so blinded by hatred for each other they don't care that their child feels like she's caught in cannon fire. This is the reason I became an attorney. I didn't want to chase ambulances or try murder suspects. I wanted to make sure no other child was used as a pawn between two selfish people."

"So this Thomas Jefferson Ward can just decide he doesn't like that you're pregnant and single—never mind your husband died before you could have kids—and you lose the part of your job that matters most."

"Yes," she said, her voice just above a whisper.

Take care of her, Jack. Promise me.

Alex's words resonated clearly in Jack's mind—as clearly as the day Alex had spoken them from the hospital bed set up in their den.

Jack had spent the last year keeping tabs on Maddie as closely as possible. Millie often played the part of unwitting informant when he subtly pumped her for information. If Tess Callahan didn't scare the daylights out of him, he'd tap her for information, too.

Then, when faced with what he considered a crazy move, Jack had offered to become a sperm donor for Maddie. To protect her, he'd told himself. No one would've known. Well, tonight he'd learned that Tess was in on the plan, and Lord knows that fact made him more than a little antsy.

Take care of her, Jack. Promise me.

Jack shut his eyes, willing the voice to go away. Willing the rogue plan beginning to formulate in his brain to stop formulating. It was a ridiculous idea. One he was sure Maddie would never agree to. But maybe, if she saw it as a way to save the work she was so obviously passionate about…

That was the only reason Jack even considered it. He'd seen the pain in Maddie's eyes. Heard the anguish in her voice. It didn't have to be "'til death do us part," even though he'd questioned more than once her willingness to raise a child with no father in the picture.

Illegitimacy wasn't the stigma it had once been. And in Atlanta no one batted an eye over a single mother. No one, apparently, but Thomas Jefferson Ward.

People like him had made Jack's childhood hell. Called him a bastard and made him feel like he'd done something wrong. He'd never had an advocate fight for him, and if he had anything to do with it, the kids of Atlanta wouldn't lose the one who sat across the table from him now.

Jack chose his words carefully. "Hear me out, Maddie. I know a way for you to have a child and keep Judge Ward happy too."

Maddie's brow furrowed with confusion. "I've wracked my brain and I can't think of a single way."

"What if you had a husband? Then your conservative judge would have no reason not to appoint you. Right?"

"Right. But I don't have a husband, remember? That's why you were going to donate sperm."

Jack inhaled deeply and held the breath until his lungs burned. He forced the air out and prepared to state his case.

"You'd have a husband if you and I got married."

Maddie froze in place for several seconds before managing a choked laugh. "Married? You and me?"

"Yeah. You and me. And a baby would make three. We'd stay married long enough to satisfy Judge Ward or until the other judge came back to work. It'd be a marriage for convenience only. You get the child you want and Judge Ward has no reason to keep you from being a guardian ad whatever."

She shook her head and then stared at him again. "You're serious."

"As serious as the heart attack that sidelined your judge. Think about it, Maddie. Go home and sleep on it. Talk it over with Tess. It's the perfect solution."

* * *

Jack leaned against the fender of his pick-up in the restaurant parking lot after seeing her safely to her car and making her promise she'd call the minute she pulled into her garage.

It's perfectly crazy. Her last words repeated in his mind as he watched the taillights of her car disappear. He knew what she was probably thinking. Same thing *he* was thinking. He wasn't right for her. He was Mr. Wrong, Wrong, Wrong. The kind of man her husband wanted Jack to protect her from.

Marriage? What on earth made him think he was husband material—much less cut out to be a father?

He'd picked one hell of a way to keep a promise.

Four

Marriage? To *Jack?*

Maddie glanced at the lighted numbers on her nightstand clock. Six in the morning and she had not slept well at all. Every time she closed her eyes, her mind flooded with visions of Jack, babies, weddings and Alex. She'd tried turning on soft music to lull her to sleep. She'd tried spraying her pillow with lavender, which usually relaxed her. Around three a.m. she'd taken an over-the-counter headache tablet, hoping it would help with the tension and allow her to doze.

At five o'clock she reached to the nightstand and picked up the phone to call Jack. If she couldn't sleep, why should he? Maybe discussing it without having to look into his blue eyes would be easier. All he had to do was grin or wink and she found herself slipping under his spell and falling like Alice down the rabbit hole.

She punched the first three digits of his number and then hung up. What if he wasn't home? What if he was home and he had a woman with him? They had no legal, binding agreement of any kind yet, so Jack might be working his way through his little black book, bedding a different woman every night before he had to give up his playboy life.

Punching her pillow, she flopped back down on her side of the bed.

Her side.

It was all her side now. Even though she was alone in the king-size bed, she'd continued to sleep only on the right, the side closest to the bathroom. She'd given away all of Alex's things, but left his dresser empty, unwilling yet to encroach on what had been his space.

No clothes hung in his closet, his drawers in the bathroom contained nothing, and because she normally didn't move about much in her sleep, the sheets on the opposite side of the bed barely needed straightening each morning.

If she and Jack married… The concept sparked all sorts of questions and concerns.

By six o'clock, Maddie surrendered and crawled from the bed. Padding barefoot to the bathroom, she groaned when she peered in the mirror. Pale skin, dark smudges under her eyes and fatigue reflected back at her. This wasn't good under ordinary circumstances and was even less advantageous for a woman who hoped to get pregnant.

After splashing cold water on her face, brushing her teeth and slathering lotion over her face, she slipped into a pair of navy velour pants with a matching pullover. She ran a brush through her hair and shoved her feet into a pair of pink house slippers. They'd been a "just because" gift from Tess—an effort to cheer her up during the last few months of Alex's illness. Who wouldn't laugh at shoes with a fuzzy pink flamingo head on each foot?

Maddie straightened the sheets but didn't make the bed completely. After tossing and turning all night, she'd probably need a nap in the afternoon, if she lasted that long.

She shuffled to the kitchen, the flamingo heads bobbing with each step. She filled the coffee maker with water and scooped fresh grounds into the basket. The coffee maker gurgled and the aroma of freshly brewed French roast filled the kitchen as she shook cereal into a bowl and splashed milk onto it.

Though the house had been built in the nineteen-twenties, the entire interior had been remodeled. The architect had maintained the integrity of the original Craftsman style but added amenities like a shower with body sprays on the side walls and an overhead rain showerhead, a whole-house audio system and a kitchen that would please any chef.

Once the coffee maker gave its final hiss and fizzle, Maddie poured a cup and added sugar and milk. She hoped the strong brew would jolt her system and let her get through making the list she needed to make—her second list of pros and cons about Jack Worth in a week.

She grabbed a legal pad and a pen from the kitchen desk and sat at the kitchen table. She couldn't believe she was actually contemplating marriage to Jack. Once again, she divided the page in half and labeled the sides PRO and CON.

She concentrated on the pros first, and the first one was obvious and easy. Marrying Jack would keep her job secure. She could continue her advocacy for children, unless Judge Ward had something against working mothers. Under that she wrote "free sperm." Just as in their first arrangement, she wouldn't have to pay a clinic for sperm. Jack would still donate at the doctor's office and she'd undergo insemination shortly after.

Research indicated that two parents, providing two sources of love and two role models was the ideal family scenario. With Jack, her baby would have that—at least for as long as they remained married. She and Jack didn't love each other, but there was no animosity and there wouldn't be even when they divorced.

As Jack had stated the night before, theirs would be a marriage staged solely for the sake of convenience. A marriage to allow Maddie to achieve two dreams: help children and have a child. She noted beside this line item that she and Jack would definitely have to address the issue of how long their marriage would last.

Two parents would also mean two pairs of helping hands. A marriage partner would offer emotional and physical help with the baby. Though she intended to breastfeed, there would be plenty of baby care to go around. Or would there? Jack had never mentioned how involved he would be with diaper changes, baths and such. She added a note to address the subject with him and explain she would need his help.

She felt certain Jack would offer her money to help with the baby's expenses, but she had no intention of taking a penny from him. Her job paid well and she had insurance money and the proceeds from the sale of her half of the business. She and her baby would manage just fine.

The last item on the list was a prenuptial agreement. If she married Jack, she would insist on a prenup. She intended to remain in control of her life. She didn't think for a moment that Jack would marry her to get his hands on her money. Once Alex had become aware he wouldn't beat lymphoma, he had made sure Jack would get the business and she would receive everything else.

On the opposite side of the paper, Maddie began the list of reasons she shouldn't marry Jack. Topping that list was guilt. At some point would she feel as if she betrayed her husband's memory? And what would people think of her marrying her husband's best friend and partner? Though the "committee of they" shouldn't play a part in her decision, Maddie still had to consider the repercussions. For all its size, Atlanta could still be a small town in many ways, and the legal community was even smaller.

Her next point: How long would they be married? Would she want him in her life for the next who-knew-how many years? She knew too well the effect of staying married for the sake of a child; she'd been that child. Maddie drew a star beside that point because she absolutely didn't want her child to suffer in the same way.

Third on the list was the matter of blending two households. Not only did she and Jack have different temperaments, they'd have to live under the same roof—her roof. Jack lived in a two-bedroom loft conversion not far from the Prescott-Worth office, so there was no question about where they'd live. Maddie's house included five bedrooms and four baths, more than enough room for two people and a newborn.

The master suite was tucked into a back corner of the ground floor, complete with an en suite bath. The guest rooms took up the second floor, and she'd already picked out a room for the nursery. In a corner with windows on two sides, the bright and cheery bedroom was perfect for a child, with room for all the necessary baby furniture and accessories and plenty of space to accommodate toys as her child grew. He or she would lack for nothing, especially love.

Jack would also be on the second floor unless he… He wouldn't dare demand to share her bedroom, would he? This was a marriage of convenience, with the emphasis on convenience. Becoming bed partners was not automatically part of their arrangement. But would Jack assume it was? He was a healthy male with a healthy sex drive—or so she presumed from the number of women she had seen him with in the past. Would he understand their sham marriage did not include bedroom privileges?

She had listed his good looks among the positive points for using him as a sperm donor. But using a handsome man's sperm and having that handsome man living in the same house were two different things. She had already found herself reacting to him physically. Maybe it was because she had been without any sexual activity since Alex had become ill. Alex had been a wonderful lover, and oh God, she had to stop thinking about Jack and sex.

She jotted *fidelity* on the list and forced her mind to back away from thoughts of Jack walking around the house without a shirt or emerging from the bathroom with only a towel slung low on his hips.

Maddie added another note to address the issues of sex and fidelity with him. He wouldn't be sleeping in her bed, but she couldn't have him running around with other women either.

While having another adult in the house to share in the baby care was a plus, having Jack around all the time presented a potential problem as well. What if the baby became too attached to him? And what if he changed his mind and fought for custody once they decided to divorce? Maddie made a note to talk to Tess about whether they could include a time limit in their contract. If they didn't stay married over a certain length of time, the baby would be less likely to be hurt when Jack left.

Lastly, she listed that she'd be going through a hormonally challenged period of her life with Jack Worth living under her roof. Maddie normally didn't have PMS problems, but from what she'd read, pregnancy was another matter. She could experience morning sickness and mood swings, neither of which would be very attractive. And while the deal didn't include being attractive to Jack, no woman wanted to be unattractive on general principle.

She figured she could hide in the master suite while she banished Jack to the basement. Maybe she could even convince him to move down there. A bedroom and full bath filled the far side of the area. He'd have a separate outside entrance and a galley kitchen plus the flat-panel, high-definition television Alex had mounted on the wall. Jack could sit around in his underwear and watch sports while she vomited and cried upstairs. That should solve the bedroom dilemma and keep his towel-clad body hidden from her sight.

She put down her pen and poured herself another cup of coffee. After doctoring it to her tastes, she walked to the wall of windows, which overlooked the backyard. Already she could imagine a wooden swing set and a playhouse or fort. Because a previous owner had added on to the original house, the backyard area wasn't as large as it had once been. But it was bordered by trees and completely fenced and would be a perfect play area.

Maddie returned to the table and studied her list again. The cons definitely outnumbered the pros, but were they enough to outweigh the ability to keep her job? Was she willing to gamble her emotions for her career? Was marrying Jack-the-hottie worth the risks?

Intellectually speaking, the answer was no. No man was worth her job. But on an emotional level, Maddie wanted to rip the list from the pad, wad it in a ball and toss it in the trash. On that same emotional level she wanted it all: her job and a baby. Maybe lack of sleep clouded her judgment, but Maddie was leaning toward the emotional option, so she went with her gut and did exactly that, crumpling the list and shoving it in the kitchen waste can along with the junk mail and coffee grounds.

She'd have to tell Tess about this latest development. She felt certain that once Tess recovered from her initial shock, she'd sit Maddie down and ask her if she'd lost her ever-loving mind.

* * ** * *

When three work days had passed and Maddie still hadn't been able to meet with Tess because of their hectic schedules, she decided to drop by her friend's apartment after work. Maddie normally avoided unannounced visits, especially after she'd interrupted Tess and a man from another law firm having an early evening adventure with a can of whipped cream and a jar of Maraschino cherries. She knew, however, that Tess was currently between relationships, so she drove toward the gated complex where her friend lived. She parked along a tree-lined street bordering the development and dialed Tess on her cell phone to give her a heads-up.

Within minutes she'd been buzzed into the common area and climbed the stairs to Tess's second-floor apartment. Tess had the front door open when she arrived and shoved a glass of wine into Maddie's hand as soon as she walked in.

"I'm sorry I've been out of pocket this week. The Beyer case has kicked my ass."

Maddie set her purse on the island as she walked past the kitchen to the living room area, which was dominated by a plush burgundy leather sofa. A cream-colored throw was draped over one side and the length of the sofa was dotted with pillows in a variety of shapes and earth tones. Maddie kicked off her pumps, shoved the pillows aside, lowered herself to the sofa and sank back with a low sigh of relief.

"I heard it was bad. Did Carl Beyer really call you a two-bit left-wing whore and tear up the conference room when he found out you had a copy of his doctored financial records?" Maddie took a sip of wine and let it rest on her tongue before warming its way to her stomach.

"He did. The situation got pretty hairy for a bit until his attorney calmed him down and reminded him everything was on tape."

"Oh that will play out really well before a judge."

Tess swirled the dark liquid in her wine glass, took two sips and sighed. "I don't believe this one will go to trial now after that outburst. I'm pretty sure opposing counsel will convince his client that our settlement offer is more than acceptable as opposed to having that tape played in court."

"You go, girl!" Maddie set the wine glass on a marble-topped antique end table and curled her legs underneath her. "You have anything to eat? I skipped lunch."

While Tess raided her refrigerator and pantry, Maddie mentally rehearsed how she was going to break the news to Tess.

How'd you like to be a bridesmaid?

Too vague.

Can you clear a Friday afternoon sometime soon and meet me at Chateau Elan?

No, Tess would think they were either going on a wine-tasting trip or hitting the spa for the weekend, not that she couldn't use a good massage to work out the knots in her neck and shoulders.

"What's bugging you?" Tess set a plate of cheese, crackers and fruit on the coffee table and grabbed a piece of pepper jack for herself. "Did you tell Jack about Judge Ward yet?" she asked, settling into an overstuffed chair.

"Yeah. We had dinner Friday night."

"I'm sure Jack wasn't heartbroken. I still can't believe he offered. Now if he'd offered to give you sperm the old-fashioned way..." Tess grinned mischievously.

"Oh Tess. Please. Not on an empty stomach." Maddie squished a piece of cheese between two crackers and took a bite.

"I have one even better. It's too bad he didn't just offer to marry you because that would solve all your problems," Tess said before taking another sip of wine.

Maddie's expression stilled just as her ears began to ring and she felt a flush spread over her neck and face. No doubt she'd turned a brilliant shade of red.

Tess choked and then swiped at her mouth with the sleeve of her sweatshirt. "Oh my God! Did he ask you to marry him? And more importantly, how did you answer?"

Maddie swallowed and took a few deep breaths before she was able to reply. "Yes, he asked, but I haven't given him an answer yet."

"Why the hell not? You aren't seriously considering marrying that man, are you? I know I joked about him being hot and all that, and I absolutely wouldn't mind getting into his pants, but sweetie, he is not marriage material any way you look at it. I am ordering you to tell him no," she said firmly.

Maddie leaned forward, plucked a grape from a bunch on the plate and popped it into her mouth. She chewed carefully, contemplating her reply.

Tess's eyes widened. "You are considering it. Here, let me swear you in and then I can cross-examine you and try to break your defense. Raise your right hand and place your left hand on this." She shoved a copy of *Cosmopolitan* toward Maddie.

Maddie pulled the magazine from Tess and tossed it back on the coffee table. "I made a list of pros and cons—"

"No way can there be more reasons to marry Jack Worth than reasons not to. Show me the list."

"I can't. It's on its way to the county landfill."

"Then recite it to me." Tess walked to a small desk in the corner and pulled out a pad and pencil. Settling back into the chair, she flipped pages until she came to a blank one. "Go ahead. Tell me the all reasons you think marrying Jack is a good idea, because I honestly can't think of a single one."

Maddie rose from the sofa and walked to the French doors that opened onto Tess's miniscule balcony. She braced her hands on each side of the doorframe and stared beyond her reflection to a toddler stopping to examine every flower and shrub in the richly landscaped beds. The mother juggled a purse, diaper bag and a briefcase and gently urged her child along.

"Then tell me the reasons it's not a good idea, and I'll agree with every one of them." Tess impatiently tapped the pencil against the pad.

Maddie turned to face her friend. "It's the only way to get what I want," she said.

"You can wait until Judge Benson comes back. He won't care if you have quadruplets by four different donors as long as you do your job. You're not that old, Maddie. Just hang on for a while longer."

"Judge Benson isn't coming back. Hightower told me today. He's taking the heart attack as a sign that he should retire from the bench and enjoy his grandchildren while he's still able. Ward will serve out the remainder of Benson's term and probably run for the position in the next election."

"That doesn't mean he'll win," Tess argued.

"And I have no assurances he won't. Tess, if I wait until all the planets are aligned properly and I have a sitting judge who won't object to my being a single parent, I may be in Judge Benson's position, but without grandchildren to spoil in my retirement." She glanced back out the window and the mother and toddler were gone. "I've considered everything. I know some people will question my decision. I know we'll have some turmoil trying to live under the same roof. I've even considered that I might be putting my child in the same ugly custody situation I was in as a child, but I'm hoping you can help me keep that from happening."

Tess raked her fingers through her hair, which made the short, spiky style stand up more than before. She tossed the pad and pencil down and went to Maddie's side. Taking her by the shoulders, she leveled her green gaze at her friend. "I won't kid you, Maddie. I think you're making a huge mistake. But I also have no idea what it feels like to want a baby as much as you do. I'll support you in any way I can, and I'll draw up a prenuptial agreement and custody waiver that's tighter than Judge Ward's... Well, I won't go there. But trust me. No attorney will be able to break it."

* * *

Jack coasted the Harley Road King to a stop in Maddie's drive at exactly three minutes before two. She'd called the night before and asked him to come over so she could give him an answer to his unorthodox but sincere proposal. He guessed that if her answer had been no, she'd have delivered her decision over the telephone. But because she'd made him come to her house to tell him yes to his sperm donor offer, he hoped she was following the same pattern and intended to take him up on this offer as well.

His offer to be her sperm donor had been spontaneous, which he didn't regret. The marriage proposal, if you could even call it a proposal, had been spur of the moment, too. He knew it was a crazy idea he would most likely regret. How could the thought of uttering two little words—*I do*—make him wake up at night in a cold sweat? Because *I do* would mean he wouldn't be with any other woman as long as he and Maddie were married. Yeah, the idea of marriage was scary. But, what scared him more was not keeping his promise to Alex.

He killed the engine and used his heel to lower the kickstand into place, then pulled the full-face helmet off, snapped it into the helmet lock and smoothed down his hair. At precisely two o'clock, he rang Maddie's doorbell and waited. When she opened the door, she stepped onto the covered front porch and looked past him to the drive.

"Is that yours?" She pointed to the motorcycle as a look of disdain crossed her face.

"Yeah," he answered hesitantly.

"You never said you had a motorcycle."

"You never asked. I didn't think it was important. Anything else you want to know? You want to take a ride on it?"

"No. I don't believe I do."

"Have you ever ridden a Harley? Ever felt all that power between your legs?" He saw her almost imperceptible reaction and was overcome with an irresistible urge to push all her buttons. For some perverse reason he wanted to make the uptight lawyer squirm. "It's the engine, you know. There's uneven firing of the cylinders, which produces the rumbling, and there's no distributor. Just a single set of points so the spark plugs fire on both cylinders each time regardless of which cylinder is on the compression stroke, thereby wasting a firing. That gives it the distinctive sound. But that's probably more than you wanted to know. I've heard some women claim they experience the big O when they ride a Harley."

He watched her lips form a perfect O, and when she saw him staring at her, she snapped them shut. She marched back into her house, leaving the front door standing open and Jack feeling satisfied that he'd made her squirm. But he was decidedly uncomfortable because while he'd been pushing her buttons, a great deal of his blood supply had diverted south and now he had to deal not only with a pissed-off woman but a hard-on as well.

And the fact that he kept wondering how *he'd* feel between her legs didn't help at all.

He followed her to the kitchen where sheets of yellow paper and manila folders were spread across one end of the black wooden table. She'd also put out a plate of chocolate chip cookies—his favorite, how did she know? —and a thermal carafe of coffee on the kitchen island. Two mugs, two small plates, a sugar bowl and small pitcher were arranged on a wooden serving tray. He slung his leather jacket over the back of one chair and hesitated.

"Help yourself," she said. After she served herself, he grabbed a handful of cookies and dropped them on the remaining plate before filling a mug and adding milk. She sat at one end of the rectangular table and pointed to a napkin and spoon sitting on the opposite end. She'd deliberately placed them as far apart at the table as possible. If she was going to accept his proposal, she was certainly keeping her distance while doing so.

Maddie fiddled with the papers and asked about Millie while he munched cookies and drained his first mug of coffee. Just as he was ready to ask if she'd invited him for a tea party, she selected one of the folders and slid it halfway across the table toward him. He reached and snagged it with a fingertip. When he opened it, the words "Prenuptial Agreement" stood out across the top of the page.

He agreed with the idea of a prenup; she needed it to protect her finances and he sure as hell didn't want her friends thinking he was only after her money. Thanks to Alex's mentoring, Jack had his own money. At the beginning of their partnership, Jack had proven himself to be the king of reckless spending—buying designer clothes, financing a sports car for way too many years and opening charge accounts with every company that sent him an application.

After the first missed payments and the resulting hiked interest rates, Alex had advised him in a non-confrontational way about shopping at off-price stores, the advantages of pre-owned vehicles and the foolishness of excessive credit.

Jack never had money growing up. His mother held a series of minimum-wage jobs and they lived in a mobile home on the wrong side of the Atlanta tracks. He worked fast food jobs in high school to buy his first clunker and keep the tank filled with gas. But by the time he was eighteen, he'd flipped burgers and manned the drive-through at every major chain because his temper and smart mouth usually got him fired within a few months.

"I presume this means we're getting married," he said flatly, flipping through the pages of legalese.

"Oh, yes. I'm sorry. I should have told you that first instead of springing the paperwork on you."

Jack started to fling back a smart-ass reply but held his tongue. He'd probably pushed her buttons enough today and needed to keep things on an even keel.

"Then I guess this is in order," he said, digging a little square blue box with a silver ribbon from the inside pocket of his jacket. He walked to her side and kneeled. Flipping the box open, he displayed a two-carat rectangular cut diamond with triangular side stones, all set in platinum. Maddie stared at the ring, reaching tentatively toward it before pulling her hand back.

"I probably should have asked first, but I thought you ought to have something to prove to everyone that our engagement is real. We can take it back to Tiffany if you like. Laurent assured me it was exchangeable. I mean, if you'd rather have one of those oblong ones, it's okay."

When she remained silent, Jack frowned and set the jeweler's box on the table in front of her. "Did I do something wrong?"

"Is this sincere? Or is this the act of a guilty conscience?" Her tone was accusatory, and Jack didn't like where the conversation was headed. "Are you worried you're not taking care of me well enough?"

A sheepish look crossed his face. "Touché. I deserved that." His comments on the front porch had been out of line and he knew it. But sometimes it was way too easy to dig at her. Way too easy to watch her nostrils flare, her eyes narrow, her breathing quicken. And when she reacted like that, Jack found himself responding in kind. And he found himself wondering how she behaved in bed.

He steered his thoughts from their current destination and focused on the situation at hand. He stood and returned to his chair. "I'm going to leave the ring with you. You can return it, exchange it or keep it. I'll leave it up to you. And when the time is right—*if* the time is right—I'd like to put it on your finger so I'll at least be able to look Millie in the eye and say the proposal was a proper one."

A look of sheer panic crossed Maddie's face. "Oh God," she moaned. "How are we going to pull this off?"

Jack had given her all the time she needed to consider his proposition, to evaluate the pros and cons and come to her own decision. The wedding was for the sake of her job, and if she decided she wanted to call the whole thing off, he'd walk away right now. With the ring. He was just crass enough to take it back. Tiffany wasn't cheap, but neither was he when it came to his promise.

"If you want to do this—and I emphasize the word *if*, because you can back out any time—the only way we can pull it off is to be as real and honest about it as possible. Nobody needs to know it's only for convenience—"

"Tess knows. I had to tell her because she drew up all the paperwork." She pointed to the stack of folders. "She won't say anything. I've sworn her to secrecy and there's the whole attorney and client privilege thing too."

"You paid her to draw this stuff up when you could have done it yourself? Why?" He stared at her in astonishment.

"Conflict of interest. I don't want anybody coming back later and saying I took advantage of you."

"I know you wouldn't do that." Jack had harbored the same worries—that he'd be viewed as opportunistic. A player.

"You say that now. But in a year, two years, whenever we decide to end this, you might feel differently. Trust me, Jack. It's better this way."

Jack considered the enormity of what they were about to do and nodded in agreement. He rose and retrieved the tray of coffee things and brought it back to the table. He held out the carafe, his eyebrows quirking questioningly.

When she refused, he refilled his cup. "I guess we should get started with the details," he said, tapping the prenuptial agreement with one finger. "Are there any surprises in here I should know about?"

"Surprises?"

"Yeah, like making me sell the Harley or making the cabin part of—"

"Cabin? You have a cabin?" Maddie scribbled on the legal pad next to her. "You should have told me about the cabin so it doesn't get mixed up in the marital property. Why didn't you tell me about it?"

"I guess the same reason I didn't tell you about the bike," he snapped. "You never asked."

Maddie blew out a long breath. "Okay. I deserved that." She scribbled more then leveled her gaze at him. "I want this to be as fair as possible. What's mine is mine and what's yours is yours."

"And what happens in Vegas stays in Vegas?" he quipped.

"Be serious, Jack."

"I am. Speaking of Vegas, just where are we going to get married? We can do it at the courthouse or drive up to Gatlinburg and get married in the mountains if you want to. Or we can fly to Vegas and get married by one of those Elvis impersonators. I mean, why not have a little fun with it?"

Jack saw the muscle in her jaw twitch and waited for the inevitable.

"Whatever we do, it has to appear to be in character, though Lord knows an Elvis wedding in Vegas might actually *be* in character for you." She pinned him with a scathing glare.

"Nah, I'm more of a Grand Ole Opry kind of guy. Maybe we could get married in the Ryman—"

"I want to avoid the courthouse," she continued, chopping him off mid-sentence, "because we shouldn't get married in the midst of every judge and lawyer in the county."

"Fair enough. How about Gatlinburg? It's nice this time of year and we can get a log cabin with a hot tub that has a view of the mountains—"

"Read my lips, Jack. This isn't a real marriage, so we don't need a honeymoon."

"But you said we have to make everyone believe it *is* a real marriage, and what better way than a honeymoon?"

Maddie tapped her pen against the table as she contemplated his suggestion. "As much as it pains me to admit it, I think you're right. But we don't have to travel that far. We can just check into a suite at the Georgian Terrace and spend a couple nights. Nobody will know we didn't go to some exotic location."

Jack slumped in his chair. The woman was hell-bent on taking every bit of the fun out of playing at being married.

"We still haven't decided where we'll get married." Jack would play by her rules if it killed him. Nobody ever guaranteed that a promise would be easy to keep.

"A friend of a friend is the wedding planner at Primrose Cottage. If we do this on a weekday, I'll bet they could work us in fairly easily. All we need is a justice of the peace and one of Primrose's small rooms that'll be big enough for you and me and two witnesses. And that reminds me. You need to line up someone to be there as a witness. I hope you don't mind, but I've asked Tess. Do you have anyone in mind?" she asked as she continued writing on her pad.

Jack narrowed his eyes, deep in thought. Alex had been his best friend and the man he'd have asked to stand beside him if he'd ever said "I do." Of course, that option no longer existed. And since he'd been running the entire operation for the past eighteen months, he'd lost contact with some of his old drinking and softball buddies. He doubted, however, that Maddie would have wanted long-haired Geoff or Tony, the consummate deer hunter, to be in her wedding. Hell, Jack wasn't sure he'd want them either.

So who? Who did he trust enough to sign his name on a marriage license? Who did he think would come to the wedding and not laugh his ass off at the idea of Jack Worth tying the knot?

Suddenly the answer was painfully clear. Not a him, but a her. Millie.

After she recovered from the shock and after he convinced her that yes, he and her former boss's widow were madly in love and couldn't live without each other, she'd willingly agree to be his "best man."

Of course, there was the matter of her having spotted him on the sperm bank website. Maybe she wouldn't connect the dots.

"Yeah, I have someone. But I'll need to ask her."

"Her?" Maddie's eyebrows nearly disappeared into her hairline. "You're going to ask one of your bimbo ex-girlfriends to be in my wedding?"

"It's my wedding, too." He clutched his hand against his chest in mock pain. "I'm wounded, Maddie, and Millie will be too when she finds out you called her a bimbo." He threw back his head and laughed.

"Millie. Well, it makes sense, and because she's a romantic at heart, she'll believe the whole thing is real. Okay, so Millie and Tess will be our witnesses."

Ninety minutes later Maddie had filled a page with pre-wedding tasks and Jack had drunk more coffee than he'd consumed in the last year.

"Okay," she said, placing her pen on the table. "We've handled the prenuptial and decided on a date and place. I'll meet you at three-thirty Monday at the probate office downtown and we can get the marriage license. Are you sure you don't want to take the premarital education classes and get the reduced-fee license?"

Jack was ready to send another barb her way, but when she grinned, he knew he'd been had. So she could dish it out, too. He'd have to file that little fact away.

"Next on the agenda is this contract." She pulled another folder from the pile and slid it to him. "It outlines the duration of our marriage, waives your right to custody and decrees that, at the time our divorce is final, the child will drop your surname and take the name Prescott. You're under no financial obligation for this child. I won't ask for child support. It'll be just like our sperm donation contract would have been. You're just providing bodily fluids, not a commitment to parenthood."

It took a moment for Maddie's last statement to sink in, and when it did, Jack closed the folder and shoved it forcibly back across the table.

"No." The single word reverberated through the room.

"No? Which part do you have a problem with? I'll get Tess to change it."

"The whole damn thing." Jack ground his teeth until he thought his jaw would crack.

"But I thought this was what you wanted. You have no responsibility and no obligation."

"And when we go our merry way, the kid doesn't have my name either. I didn't know the truth about my father until I was eighteen years old and I won't be a part of having any kid being called a bastard."

"But that won't be the case. You'll be listed on the birth certificate."

"Yeah, but apparently I disappear from the record book when we split and I refuse to put any child in the position of appearing to be illegitimate. I'll waive custody but I'll support my child." He spoke with determination. "And about those bodily fluids. Just how are you planning to get pregnant after we're married?"

"The same way I was going to get pregnant before. Artificial insemination with your sperm."

Jack steepled his fingers under his chin and pressed his index fingers to his lips. Then he lowered his hands to the table and laid them flat, his fingers spread wide.

"No," he repeated.

"How else am I supposed to get pregnant?"

"Don't you think it'll look a little peculiar if you get pregnant by artificial insemination when we haven't been married long enough to know whether the old-fashioned way even works or not?"

Maddie's eyes widened and Jack could see he'd hit a nerve with the thought. "Nobody has to know."

"Get real, Maddie. For all its millions of people, Atlanta is still a small southern town at heart and everybody knows everybody else's business. One careless slip of the tongue and everybody will think my little swimmers aren't good enough and you had to pick a donor daddy and use a turkey baster to get pregnant."

"So this is about your *swimmers*?" she asked cynically. "Your ego is bruised?"

"That wasn't my intent, and you know it. But now that you mention it, I do have a reputation to maintain and my swimmers would like Michael Phelps to know he has stiff competition. No pun intended." Jack stifled the urge to laugh.

"You aren't honestly suggesting I get pregnant by—"

"The old-fashioned way? That's exactly what I'm suggesting. After all, I'm just an old-fashioned kind of guy. Besides, it's cheaper that way. You can save your money for Junior's college fund."

"But I can't have sex with you." Maddie's voice rose an octave. "What will people think?"

"Nobody has to know," he said in a sing-song voice, repeating her earlier words.

"Get real, Jack," she replied. Jack saw the moment she realized they were replaying the previous argument in reverse.

They stared at each other and he could practically see the wheels turning in her head.

Finally Maddie shrugged. "We do it only when I ovulate." She capitulated and ground out the words between clenched teeth.

As much as he'd love to be in her bed every night, he wouldn't push her now. "Okay. That's when it matters."

"And you sleep in the guest room."

"I wouldn't have it any other way."

Of course he'd sleep in the guest room. No way would he sleep in Alex's bed.

"That just leaves one thing," she said, pointing to her list. "We need to set a date. If I can get Primrose, is next Friday okay with you?"

Jack gulped. Next Friday? Could he accomplish what he needed in less than a week? Aw, hell yes. If she could arrange a whole wedding, he could dig his suit out of the closet and show up. But there was one more item—not on her agenda but on his.

He strode to the opposite end of the table, eased the ring from the blue and silver box and knelt again. His first inclination was to ask Maddie if she wanted to run off and get hitched.

Then he saw her gaze at the ring, her expression softening.

Take care of her.

This was no time for jokes. He took her left hand in his and poised the ring at the end of her fourth finger.

"Madelyn Prescott, will you marry me?"

Her affirmative answer was little more than a whisper, but whispered or shouted, she'd said "Yes." Jack slipped the ring past her knuckle until it rested snugly on her finger.

For one moment he wished the marriage was real. Wished they'd be going on a week-long honeymoon to a remote location. Wished they'd be sharing a bed and making love every night.

Despite his jokes and the talk of their convenient marriage, the idea of being a real husband to this woman had grown appealing beyond just the sexual aspect. And that shook him to his core. He wasn't real husband material. He didn't come from that kind of family. Didn't know what a real marriage was supposed to be beyond what he had seen with Alex and Maddie.

Take care of her.

The voice in his head reeled him back to reality. He rose off bended knee and moved quietly toward the foyer, pulling on his jacket as he did.

"I'll let myself out," he said.

She nodded, her back toward him and her left hand still outstretched with the diamond ring sparkling in the light.

The last time he'd walked out of Maddie Prescott's kitchen, she'd said "okay." This time she was about to say "I do," and so was he.

Five

Maddie glanced up as her office door creaked open and Tess poked her head in.

"Busy?"

She closed the computer document she'd been slaving over since she'd returned from getting the marriage license with Jack, and she minimized the screen. "Not too busy for you. I'm surprised you're still here. It's..." Maddie glanced at her wristwatch.

Tess squeezed between the door and the frame then eased the door closed. "It's way past time to go home, but here it is." She clutched a sheaf of papers tightly, as if reluctant to hand them over. "Are you...?"

"Sure? Dammit, Tess. Don't ask me that question again. Of course I'm sure. What choice do I have?"

Tess eased into the straight-backed chair across the desk from her friend. "Honey, you have lots of choices. I simply do not want to see you screw up your life and your career by marrying this...this..."

"This what? I thought you said he was a hunk. I thought you said you'd debrief him in a moment. Why is it okay for you to think he's great, but the mistake of the century if I marry him?"

"It's only been a year since Alex died. Are you sure you're not just acting from grief? I know you guys wanted to have kids and all, but are you sure you're not rushing into this marriage with Jack?"

Maddie laughed bitterly. "My mother only waited two months after divorcing my father before she remarried."

And her new stepfather had waited less than ten days to make a pass at Maddie. He'd grabbed her from behind and the only thing that had stopped him from doing more than copping a feel was the sound of the housekeeper's footsteps in the hallway.

Maddie had made a point of never being alone with Devin after that. She'd never said a word to anyone, but her mother's housekeeper, Lucille, knew intuitively to protect her.

Of course, Lucille couldn't protect her when she finally told her biological father and he dragged her mother back into court, screaming foul over the new husband, the custody order and the child support payments. Bradley Yates didn't want custody of his only child; his job as public relations manager for some of country music's biggest stars took him all over the world. He simply wanted to please his bimbo du jour, and that usually meant making his ex-wife miserable.

And along with that came misery for an innocent twelve-year-old girl who was bounced back and forth from a mansion in the Nashville suburb of Brentwood to a lakefront house on Old Hickory Lake thirty miles away.

"So don't make the same mistake your mother did," Tess said.

"Is that what you think? That I'm making a mistake?"

Tess released a long, audible breath. "We've known each other since we were fresh out of law school and rookies at the firm. We've been through a lot together and I don't think I can stand to watch you get hurt again."

"Jack won't deliberately hurt me. He's not that kind of person."

"Alex didn't set out to hurt you either, but he did. He got sick and he died, and all the happiness you had in your life was destroyed. You never smiled and you hid inside that great big house. All you did was work. And now you're going to marry a man you don't love so you can work some more." Tess leaned forward, her gaze steady and her chin up. "I'll go with you on Friday and I'll stand beside you. And if anyone asks me, I'll tell them you're the happiest married woman in the state of Georgia. But I swear, if Jack Worth hurts you, I'll…I'll…"

"You'll say *I told you so.*" Maddie's voice was flat.

"No, I'll hurt him. He will be missing a few very vital male body parts."

Maddie laughed out loud. "I know it's not funny, but you'd do that." Then she sobered again and stood, walked to her office window and stared at her vague reflection in the glass.

"I loved Alex the moment I met him. He was handsome and funny and smart, and he made me feel beautiful and sexy and like I was the only person on earth. I thought we'd be together forever. But forever has a way of coming too soon sometimes."

I missed it, Maddie—kids, car pools, Little League, AARP. All of it. I thought I could have it all. That we could have it all. Don't make the same mistake. Please. Promise me you won't let life pass you by.

"Alex wanted children right away because he was ten years older than me, but I held back. I regret the decision now. A child would have been someone to keep on loving."

"So this is about something to love? You could get some goldfish for crying out loud." Tess shook her head in dismay.

Maddie turned, sent Tess a chilling look and returned to her desk. "I don't expect you to understand. You're career-oriented all the way. Your uterus isn't ticking like mine. And I respect that, Tess. Please try to understand my feelings and respect them." She took the papers Tess had prepared and dropped them into her briefcase where they settled next to the marriage license. "I'll look these over tonight, though I'm sure everything's in order."

Tess rose without a word and walked to the door.

"I don't want this to drive a wedge between us, Tess. I married the first time for love and I'm not sure I'll ever get a chance like that again. But Jack's a decent man and it's going to be all right. You have to believe me."

Tess remained by the door, motionless, posture erect. Just when Maddie thought the wedge might have already been driven, Tess's shoulders slumped a little.

"I do," she said just before leaving Maddie's office.

This marriage with Jack was different. It was safe, and no L-O-V-E was involved or even allowed. The rules were defined up front.

So why did she alternate between excitement and apprehension? Guilt one moment and believing she was doing the right thing just seconds later? She needed to believe her own words: everything would be all right. She'd get a baby to love and love her back. And Jack could say he'd kept his promise to Alex—in spades.

* * *

The parking lot of the Rosebud Diner still had empty parking spaces when Jack steered Millie's matronly sedan into one at the end of a row. They'd driven her car because his truck was covered in red dust, not to mention coffee cups, burger wrappers and stray French fries filled the passenger seat and an old Krispy Kreme box lay crushed on the floorboard. He'd meant to take the truck through the car wash but his day, not to mention his thoughts, had been filled with wedding plans.

The hostess ushered them to a pink Formica and chrome table in the corner. Short on ambience but long on kitsch, the color scheme left patrons feeling like they were dining inside a bottle of Pepto Bismol. Décor aside, the diner served the best meatloaf in the city and their cornbread would melt right on your tongue.

Jack had discovered the Rosebud when he'd worked on a remodeling job nearby, in the days before the Atlanta lovelies had pounced on it and added it to their list of "must visit" restaurants. Now the parking lot was as apt to be filled with Hummers and Jags as with pickups and family sedans. That's why Jack and Millie had come straight from work. He'd hoped to avoid the frantic rush of the evening tourist crowd.

Wedding plans topped the list of things he needed to discuss tonight, and the receipt from the marriage license bureau burned in his pocket as a constant reminder of the week's upcoming event. But first he'd satisfy Millie's appetite with the best down-home southern cuisine the city had to offer, and then he'd ask about her granddaughter and Wolfgang, the black Lab-Great Dane mix that might as well be her third grandchild. Hell, he might even get her good and juiced before he told her.

The hostess handed them each a menu. "Y'all's waitress is fixin' to come over here and take your drink orders. My name's Shelby Lynn and your waitress is Crystal. Just let me know if there's anything we can get y'all, okay?"

"You can get the bartender to fix me a scotch and soda for starters," Millie replied, exhaustion apparent in her tone.

When the hostess cast a sympathetic look in Jack's direction, he merely smiled and ordered a beer.

After their waitress had delivered their drinks and taken their food orders, Millie sipped her scotch and fixed Jack with the pointed stare he'd grown used to over the years. "What's going on?"

"What's going on?" Jack parroted. "Not much really."
Liar.

Millie narrowed her eyes then unrolled her silverware and smoothed the white cloth napkin in her lap.

"You've been jumpy all day, you disappeared this afternoon when I know for a fact you had two proposals to work on and you brought me here to the pink palace for dinner. You don't fool me for a minute."

Jack took a long drink from his beer and surreptitiously studied Millie over the rim of the glass. Her steely gray gaze stared back, letting him know she was not only on to his little avoidance tactic, but she'd hound him until he came clean.

"Can I at least wait until after we eat?" he asked as the server slid a plate of meatloaf, mashed potatoes and fried okra in front of him.

Millie leaned over her meal of fried chicken, fried green tomatoes and collard greens and inhaled deeply. "If you're worried about killing my appetite, let me clue you in on something. I raised two boys of my own and I'm not sure there's anything that could surprise me now."

"I wouldn't be so sure about that," Jack mumbled, shaking pepper over his plate before forking mashed potatoes into his mouth.

"Well I wouldn't want a growing boy like you to miss his supper, so let's eat and we'll talk later." She picked up a crispy drumstick, bit off a piece and chewed. "Oh, my heavens. Does this come with a defibrillator?" She dabbed at her lips with her napkin and left a trail of red lipstick on the material. "This will clog my arteries faster than Friday traffic clogs the downtown connector, but it is positively orgasmic."

Jack coughed and grabbed his glass of water. "Geez, Millie. Warn a guy when you're going to talk sex at the table, would you?"

Millie's throaty laugh filled the air. "Aw, honey, that's not talking sex. If you want me to talk sex, I could tell you about the time Clayton and I—"

"That's okay," Jack interrupted. "Why don't you catch me up on the family news, and I promise as soon as the waitress takes our plates away I'll tell you what's on my mind."

Millie filled him in on her teenage granddaughter's latest boyfriend, her younger son's quest to become a firefighter and how her condo homeowners' association had crossed the line by objecting to the concrete lawn art in the neighbor's front yard.

"It's a First Amendment violation," she insisted. "And I tried to tell them so. But they won't listen. Does Maddie take cases like that if Edna decides to sue?"

"Her specialty is family law, so no. I don't think she'll argue the First Amendment rights of yard stuff in court. Is it a naked statue?"

"Oh, hell no. Nothing as exciting as that. It's a bunch of concrete bunnies and ducks and such. Personally I think they're tacky, but you can't legislate good taste. It's just the principle of the whole thing."

Jack halfheartedly agreed, mulling over in his mind just how he'd break the news of his upcoming Friday nuptials and ask her to stand by his side as a witness to the whole farce.

Millie shoved her empty plate to one side, then picked up her glass and frowned at the diluted scotch in the bottom. "Time's up," she announced. "Spill it."

Jack inhaled a fortifying breath. "I took off this afternoon since I had to go get a marriage license because Maddie and I are getting married on Friday afternoon." The words whooshed out in a long stream.

A look of pure disbelief crossed Millie's face and she upended the glass and finished off her watered-down drink. "I need a refill," she demanded, holding the glass at arm's length.

"Hell, Millie, it's not that bad." He took the glass from her and set it on the empty table behind him.

"You're not seeing your face from my point of view. You look like a man who's just been sentenced to life in prison. The last time I checked, you were supposed to look happy when you're getting married."

Jack consciously tried to relax his facial muscles and remove the apparent image of combined panic and dread.

Millie grabbed the waitress's arm as she passed by and asked for two cups of coffee. "I want the whole story. Right now. Why are the two of you getting married and why so soon?"

Jack paused, unsure how to answer her.

"Oh shit, Jack. You didn't get her pregnant, did you?"

"Has anybody ever told you that you cuss too much?"

"Don't change the damn subject. Did you get her pregnant?"

"Well, not exactly."

"Either you did or you didn't. You can't be partly pregnant."

Over coffee, Jack relayed the whole story—from "I will donate sperm" to "will you marry me" and everything in between. Millie sat speechless; it was the only time Jack could remember the woman not having an acerbic reply.

"I do have a favor to ask."

"Am I going to need another drink?" she asked.

"I don't know. Maybe."

"Oh, just go ahead and ask. After what you've just told me, I don't know that anything could shock me now."

Jack wondered why he thought Millie would be stunned if he asked her to stand beside him when he took Maddie to be his lawfully wedded wife. Maybe because in the early years, when he'd first started working for Alex, Millie was more likely to have to stand beside him while he explained to Alex why he'd come in hung over again. Or why getting off early on Friday afternoon to get ready for a hot date was his idea of emergency leave.

"I need to bring a witness to the ceremony. And well, I wanted to ask you if you'd come with me."

"Do you *need* me?" Millie asked, her voice softening. "Or do you want me to be there?"

Jack thought a moment. "To be honest, both. We don't need witnesses to sign the marriage license, but given the circumstances, Maddie and I believe we need a couple of people who can vouch that we really did get married. That we're not just pretending." He cupped the coffee mug in his hand, drawing warmth from it. "This whole thing has me scared to death, but I made a promise and I'm just trying the best I know how to keep it. It'd mean a lot to me, and to Maddie, too, if you were there to sort of give us your blessing."

Jack watched the features on Millie's face soften. "I'd be honored."

Thirty minutes later she stood beside him in the men's department of Neiman Marcus. When she'd asked what he planned to wear to the wedding, and he'd told her, she ordered him to drive to the mall and had practically frog-marched him into the pricey store.

"I am not paying two hundred and twenty-five dollars for a noose," Jack proclaimed as she held a gray Armani tie in one hand and a red striped one in the other.

"You told me yourself you needed to make sure this looked like a real wedding."

"It *is* a real wedding."

"Let me put it another way. You need to make this look like a real *marriage*. Like two people in love. Two people who care enough about each other to dress for the part."

"I'll have on my charcoal gray suit." It was the suit he'd purchased for Alex's funeral. "And I have a white shirt that's still in the plastic bag from the laundry. Can't I wear one of the ties I already have?"

"A tie with Barney Fife's face in the middle is not appropriate for a wedding, and neither is one that looks like the blueprints for a house."

"I already have a red striped one," he began, pointing to the one she held.

"And the last time I saw you wear it, it had a gravy stain right in the middle. And before you try to argue with me, ties don't dry clean well. If I know Maddie, she's invested a lot of time and effort into the way she's going to look. Trust me, Jack," she said, pressing the Armani into his hands. "Buy the tie. You won't regret it."

* * *

The following afternoon, Maddie groaned under the weight of a cardboard box. "What do you have in here?" She set it back on the tailgate of Jack's pickup and wiped perspiration off her forehead with the tail of her t-shirt. When she reached to pick it up again, Jack stepped in and grabbed it away, lifting it to his shoulder as if it weighed nothing.

"I said you didn't have to carry those boxes. I'm perfectly capable of doing my own lifting and toting. Don't you have bride stuff to take care of?"

"Nope," she said, flopping onto the bottom porch step. She reached for a bottle of water, unscrewed the cap and tilted her head back to drink, allowing the cool water to quench her thirst. "Tess has taken care of everything. Pretty much all I have to do is show up on Friday. How about you?"

"All my bride stuff is taken care of, too."

Maddie tossed the bottle cap at him and grinned. "You know what I mean."

Jack carried the last box inside then returned to the small deck off the basement area with a cold can of beer. He settled onto the step beside her. "Millie has been a real sweetheart. She's arranged everything and won't even let me pay her overtime. She said she never got to be the mother of the groom."

"But her son is married."

"Yeah, but Clay and Vanessa eloped." He popped the top on the can and took a long drink, his throat muscles working as he swallowed. "And after dealing with Hurricane Millie I can just about understand why. She has this clipboard and a bunch of folders with wedding stuff in them. She called me at eleven-thirty last night to ask me if I needed her to handle our honeymoon arrangements."

"What did you tell her?" Maddie asked, her voice calm in an attempt to camouflage her panic.

"I told her I'd already taken care of it. That we had a suite at a hotel in town because we can't both take off work right now. But that we'd probably take a nice trip sometime later."

Maddie felt relief replace the panic. Millie knew why they were getting married: to get Maddie pregnant. But she didn't have to know the intimate details. It was none of her business that Jack planned to sleep on the sofa in the suite at the Georgian Terrace while she spent her wedding night alone in the bed. It was also none of her business that Jack would be taking over the basement area of Maddie's house instead of sharing her bedroom—and her bed.

They had decided the basement was a better option than the guest room. He'd stash enough of his belongings in Maddie's bedroom and bathroom to convince people he lived there. There'd be beer in the refrigerator, aftershave in the bathroom and if it would help paint the picture of wedded bliss, she'd leave one of his t-shirts on the recliner in the den.

Downstairs, he'd have a bedroom, bathroom, galley kitchen and living area with a separate entrance; a stairway at one end of the living area led to the first floor. The large, flat-panel TV and wet bar in the basement provided the perfect getaway for any husband, especially one who wasn't sleeping with his wife.

Jack finished his beer and crushed the can in his hand. "Ready to help me unpack?" He stood and held out a hand to her.

"I thought you just told me you didn't need me to help you move."

"Move, yeah. Unpacking is something else. Since there's no unpacking fairy, you've been tapped to help me decide where to put my underwear and socks."

Jack led the way through the furnished living area, past the leather sofa, around the game table and into the room Maddie had been using for off-season clothes storage. Now a warm brown burled wood king-size sleigh bed dominated the room. Bands of inlaid wood in the headboard and footboard created a subtle pattern, and brushed nickel accents added a modern touch. A matching nightstand sat beside the bed with only a lamp and alarm clock on it. A tall chest stood against one wall.

A thick chocolate-and-rust-plaid duvet covered the mattress, and a rust bed skirt hung to the floor. Rust-colored pillows rested against the headboard and a handful of smaller pillows in coordinating colors lined up in front of them.

Jack had also moved in a brown-and-tan-striped upholstered chair with a sage-green, chunky-knit throw draped across the back of it. The room certainly looked different than when she'd left for work that morning. Jack had left Millie to man the office and deal with the university professor who was going to rent his condo. He'd used the day to finish packing and move what he wasn't putting in storage.

"It's too girly," he stated, leaning against the closet door. "I told the decorator I wanted something nice but not too...too..." His voice trailed away.

"Girly?"

"I'll call her tomorrow and tell her to pick it up and find me something else that's more masculine. Something like...oh..."

"Camouflage? Superheroes?"

"Very funny. I bet even your bedroom doesn't look this froofy."

"Actually, I think this is quite nice. It's understated but contemporary. It's not girly at all."

"Really? I kinda thought maybe all those little pillows were a bit much." He waved his hand in the general direction of the bed.

She shook her head. "If they all represented different baseball teams, then they'd be too much."

"You're sure?" he asked, giving her an appraising look.

"Positive. And why did you hire a decorator? Why didn't you just bring what you had at your condo?"

"My condo is the epitome of understated bachelor. I don't own a bedspread, much less half a dozen froofy little pillows. I found a professor at Tech to rent it and he wanted it furnished if possible. So I went out to a furniture store, bought this bedroom stuff and the decorator sort of came with the deal. And you're sure this stuff looks okay, 'cause I don't want to mess up your decorating scheme. I took some pictures of the house with my cell phone and showed Suzanne. She's the decorator."

"Sugarbaker?" Maddie asked, trying her best to keep a straight face.

"Who?" Jack asked, a puzzled look on his face.

"Never mind. Stop worrying about the room. It's good. Really. I'll show you my room one day and you can see what girly really is." She regretted the offer as soon as she'd made it, and the awkwardness caused her cheeks to flush.

"You know, we never have really talked about when or where we'll do it." Jack walked to the bed, sat on the edge and bounced a bit. He patted the plaid material beside him. "Come here."

Hesitantly, Maddie crossed the room and eased down beside him. She'd been so preoccupied with wedding details she hadn't had time to contemplate the particulars of their pregnancy negotiation. Having sex with Jack in her bed was out of the question. And having sex here would definitely give him the home-court advantage. Their arrangement would have been so much easier if Judge Benson hadn't suffered a heart attack.

"Is something wrong?" he asked softly.

"Other than the fact I'm marrying my late husband's best friend in three days?" Immediately she realized the gravity of her statement.

Jack angled toward her and took her hands in his. He rubbed his thumb over her engagement ring. "Maddie, if you think any part of this arrangement is wrong, we can stop it right now. We'll cancel Primrose Cottage, we'll tear up the marriage license, and I'll call off Millie."

She blinked back tears and Jack pulled her to him, putting his arm around her. Her head rested on his shoulder. This was the first time they'd had any sort of body contact since Jack had hugged her awkwardly at Alex's funeral. Late-afternoon stubble darkened his jaw and the citrusy musk of his cologne tickled her nose. She breathed in the scent and relaxed into his embrace.

This was what she missed: the companionable contact, the chit-chat over dinner, the knowledge that someone else was there. She had wandered around her large house for a year and having Jack here already made things seem right again.

"I didn't mean it that way," she apologized, taking in another whiff of his masculine smell. "It's just nerves. Stress."

"PMS?" he asked with a hesitant note in his voice.

Maddie laughed and Jack hugged her tighter. "I don't get PMS, and I have a pretty regular cycle."

"I read all the stuff on the website about cycles and hormones and taking your temperature every morning. I won't try to tell you that I understood it all, but if you'll just give me a little shove in the right direction, I'll work with you."

She laughed again and leaned away from him. "There are ways for me to determine when I ovulate. We'll just plan to uh…be together that night."

"So what kind of time frame are we talking about?" he asked. "In regard to you ovulating that is. A couple of days? A week?"

"About ten days or so," she told him.

Ten days to get settled into her new life. Ten days to get used to having Jack around the house. Ten days until she would have sex with him, and strangely, that thought sent a little zing straight to her middle—perhaps for no other reason than she'd been celibate for so long.

"Just let me know when and where." He winked and Maddie felt that little zing again, only it traveled further this time.

Nerves. That's all it was.

"I guess we better get the rest of my stuff unpacked. And don't worry about dinner. I already called in an order for pizza."

* * *

Three days later, Jack stood in a sunny fifteen-by-fifteen room at Primrose Cottage and exchanged pleasantries with the justice of the peace. This wasn't a tux and bridal gown wedding. Jack would have been happy to say "I do" wearing jeans and his favorite t-shirt, but he and Maddie would need wedding photos to prove they were actually married, and who would believe Jack Worth was married if they saw him standing in front of a justice of the peace in jeans and a t-shirt? Hell, who would believe he was married, period? He tugged the collar of the starched white dress shirt and smoothed the gray Armani tie from Neiman Marcus.

Two hundred and twenty-five dollars. Damn.

It's not that he couldn't afford it; he just normally wouldn't *want* to afford it. But Millie had a point about looking the part. Add the cost of the tie to the two-carat rock from Tiffany and the two-night stay in a suite at the Georgian Terrace, and he had a dent the size of Cincinnati in his bank account. By Monday lots of folks should be believing Jack Worth was really married.

Millie slipped into the room and made her way toward Jack. She had dressed the part, too. The hem of her black dress hit below her knees and the top was dotted with beads and sequins. She wobbled in a pair of too-high heels, and diamond studs sparkled in her earlobes.

"I thought people wore black to funerals," Jack whispered once she reached his side.

"Hush or I'll be wearing this to yours when Maddie finds out you're being a smart ass."

"Yes ma'am." Today Jack would behave. He'd be the adoring fiancé and once he said "I do" he would be husband everyone expected him to be. Or at least he would be in public.

The justice of the peace cleared his throat and nodded toward the opposite end of the room. The door opened and Tess stepped in wearing a long black dress and carrying a bouquet of blood red roses.

"More funeral attire?" he murmured. "Is this some sort of message?"

Millie hushed him again then directed his attention back to Tess who turned and smiled, and continued into the room, followed by Maddie.

Jack heard Millie's quick intake of breath and then he got his first glimpse of the bride. *His bride.* Elegant in its simplicity, Maddie's off-white dress brushed the floor as she walked to the makeshift altar. She wore no veil and her only accessories were a strand of pearls and matching earrings.

As she neared, Jack realized his hands were clenched and he'd held his breath. He sucked in air and felt his chest expand, tugging at his shirt buttons. Maddie stared straight ahead, looking at the back of Tess's head. When she reached his side, Jack opened his mouth to comment and found himself speechless. He couldn't believe what he saw, couldn't believe just how beautiful this woman was.

She passed her bouquet of cream-colored roses to Tess and cast a tentative glance in his direction. The justice of the peace began to speak and Jack focused his attention on the words. They vowed to honor and trust and to stand by each other through the tides of change. At the appropriate time, Millie placed a simple platinum band in his palm and he slipped it onto Maddie's finger. He watched his own hand tremble when he held it out to receive a ring from Maddie. Taking a deep breath, he tensed the muscles in his arm and willed the trembling to stop as she slid a ring onto his finger.

"By the power vested in me by the state of Georgia, I now pronounce you husband and wife."

Maddie's eyes glistened and Jack wanted more than anything to make her believe she had not made a mistake by accepting his offer of marriage.

"You may kiss your bride."

He could kiss his bride.

Jack gently pulled her close and framed her face with his palms. Slowly, but deliberately he tilted her face upward as he lowered his mouth to hers. The kiss went from sweet and warm to red hot and blazing in a matter of seconds. He ran his tongue lightly along the seam of her lips, asking for entrance, and when she opened to him, he tenderly nibbled on her lower lip. His body responded—pulse quickening, breath lodging in his chest, body hardening from the sheer emotion.

He reined in the kiss, promising himself it would never happen again—at least not so passionately. He'd have to kiss Maddie again; it would be part of their act. He'd limit it to tender pecks on her cheek or a quick brush of his lips against hers. One thing was for certain, he acknowledged something for Maddie that hadn't been there before.

It wasn't love, but it was sure as hell more than just like.

He was starting to worry about their honeymoon, and he hoped the Georgian Terrace had a good supply of cold water.

Six

Jack had turned off the ringer on his desk phone and left Millie with strict orders not to disturb him—unless it was Maddie calling. Since their wedding, Jack had settled into his basement bachelor quarters and Maddie seemed to tiptoe around him even more tenuously than before they were married.

They rarely saw each other on weekday mornings. Jack rose early and worked out on the elliptical trainer he'd moved from his condo. After showering, he'd grab an energy bar or nuke a frozen breakfast sandwich and head for work. If he was lucky, Millie beat him to the office and had the coffee brewed by the time he arrived. If he was very lucky, she'd see his truck pull into the parking lot and have a cup ready for him to grab as he walked past her desk and into his office.

Shortly into their marriage, he'd worked late and arrived home to find a plate with cold steak and a soggy baked potato on the kitchen table. Maddie had delivered a talk on common courtesy and they had come to an understanding. He'd also eaten the steak and potato, and he'd been home on time every night since or let her know he'd be late.

How ironic that the night he'd spotted the letter from the sperm bank he'd been planning to call an end to their monthly dinners. Now they sat across from each other at the same table and discussed everything but the event due to happen any day.

She had explained how the ovulation test worked and that once it indicated a hormone surge, they should have sex within forty-eight hours. Jack wasn't used to sex on a schedule and found the idea unsettling to say the least. Sex should be spontaneous and fun. And when Jack had had a sex life, before Alex became too ill to run the company, that's exactly the way his had been—spur of the moment and pure pleasure.

Now he was on call, waiting for the phone to ring and hoping that when he was called on to perform according to a timetable and with a woman who was his wife but not his lover, the mind-body connection wouldn't short-circuit and go on the blink.

Performance had never been an issue. Not the first time when he was a high school sophomore in the backseat of senior Angela

Norton's father's new Buick Electra, and not the last time with Barbie Whatever halfway through Alex's illness when he learned the bone marrow transplant hadn't worked. She had been willing and available, and while Jack wasn't particularly proud of that incident, his equipment had still been in perfect operating condition. He had dated other women since Barbie, but the pressure of carrying the full load at Prescott-Worth often had him falling asleep before he and his date could get much beyond a kiss.

"The phone's for you, boss. It's Maddie." Millie stood in the doorway and frowned at him. "Didn't you hear me?"

"Sorry, no. I was distracted," he explained.

"You've been distracted a lot this week. Everything's okay at home, isn't it?"

"Yeah, everything's fine," he said, reaching for the phone. "Would you close the door on your way out?"

He took a fortifying breath before picking up the receiver and saying hello. And he breathed a sigh of relief when Maddie had nothing to report. God, wouldn't the guys on the job site have a field day if they knew he wasn't bonking his wife nightly?

"Call me when something surges," he told her, adding he'd be home around six and would bring takeout from their favorite Thai restaurant. She was stressed enough without adding cooking to the mix.

He hung up the phone and returned to the spreadsheet on his computer. He'd only made three entries when the door swung open and Millie entered with two glasses of what appeared to be fruit juice.

"Here," she said, thrusting the glass into his hand. "I fixed you something cold to drink."

Jack eyed her suspiciously, curious about the unusual afternoon refreshments. He lifted the glass to his lips, took a big sip and struggled for breath as the liquid burned all the way to his stomach.

"Holy hell! Why didn't you tell me you'd spiked it with vodka?" He wiped his mouth with the back of his hand and wheezed again. "And why did you feel the need to incinerate my esophagus?"

Millie lowered herself into the corner chair and sipped from her glass. "I thought maybe you'd like to talk about what's bugging you. And what better way to talk than over drinks?"

Jack sniffed the contents of his glass then set it to one side. "Setting fire to my vocal chords isn't the best way to get me to talk.

And I have work to do anyway." He pointed to the offending drink. "Would you take that with you when you leave?"

Millie took another swallow and crossed one leg over the other, making it quite clear to Jack she wasn't going anywhere. So he'd ignore her. Maybe she'd stop trying to make him talk and return to her desk.

Five minutes later, when she remained in his office, calmly sipping her drink, Jack admitted defeat. What the hell? He deserved a stiff drink after all he'd been through. He knocked back another swallow and swiveled the desk chair to face his busybody office manager. Craning his neck back, he stared at the ceiling.

"You want to know what's bugging me?" he offered. "I'll tell you what's bugging me. Maddie is short-tempered and about as irritable as a cat who's just had a bath. Everything I say is wrong, and if I say nothing, she wants to know why I won't talk to her. I'm scared to go home and scared not to."

"It's probably PMS."

"No, it's that damn ovulation test. It has her so frazzled she locked herself out of the house in her nightgown this morning. Luckily I was still there to let her in."

"So when's the big day? Or maybe I should say the big night?"

"If her calculations are right, and the test shows a smiley face when it's supposed to, it should be this weekend. That is, if she doesn't divorce me first."

Millie chuckled and lifted her glass. "More?"

"No, thank you. One Molotov Cocktail is enough."

"Cut her some slack. This is a big step for her. On your way home tonight, get some flowers in addition to the takeout. It'll earn you brownie points."

"How'd you know—?"

"It doesn't matter how I know about your dinner plans. But it does matter that I know how another woman feels when she's getting ready to take one of the biggest steps in her life. You need to make the weekend romantic."

"Romantic, huh?" Wouldn't Millie be surprised by their sleeping arrangements, too?

"Why don't you take her to the cabin for the weekend? Maybe a change of scenery will help. And it's certainly romantic in the mountains."

Jack nodded thoughtfully. "I think you might be right. If Maddie can take the afternoon off on Friday, consider yourself on vacation after lunch. I'll need to call Charlotte and ask her to air out the place. But I think it's perfect for a conception."

"Better yet, it's the perfect place for a seduction," Millie offered as she pushed herself to a standing position and returned to her desk.

The seed of an idea began to take root. Why not? Jack saw absolutely no reason why conceiving a child couldn't be as much pleasure as business, and he had two days to plan the perfect seduction.

* * *

Maddie's hand shook as the face indicator on the ovulation test smiled at her, almost mocking in its clarity. She pulled her cell phone from her purse and began to dial Jack. He'd told her to call when the results were positive.

But she didn't want to sound desperate, as if she couldn't wait to hop in the bed with him. This wasn't about sex; it was about a baby. And that was all. Then she remembered she was in a stall in the ladies' restroom at work, the test lying flat on top of the toilet tissue dispenser.

This was near the bottom of the list of ideal spots to learn if you were ovulating. She'd have preferred her bathroom at home, but since she had to test twice a day, she was forced to hide away in the far stall at work. Half the office probably thought she had an overactive bladder problem.

She hesitated, her fingers hovering over the phone screen, unwilling to risk having someone walk in and overhear her conversation. She was also reluctant to place herself at risk of being fodder for the office grapevine, though she suspected she already was.

Then the perfect idea formed. She touched the texting icon on her phone, typed in Jack's name and tapped three buttons before hitting send.

:-)

Surely he would know what it meant.

As she shut off the phone and reached for the test, the diamond ring on her left hand caught the light overhead. It represented more than a marriage. The ring was about a baby, too. And the job she needed to return to. She'd never have let Jack talk her into marriage if her job hadn't been at risk.

Her work was the most important part of her life now. Too many children depended on her to protect them from warring parents or addicted mothers and fathers too strung out to even feed them.

Of course, once she had a child in her life, her priorities would change. She would prove, however, she could combine a career and parenthood and be a success at both. She would move heaven and earth to make it work.

She sealed the testing apparatus in a plastic bag and dropped it into her purse, then double checked, making sure she'd picked up every scrap of packaging. She couldn't afford to leave telltale clues.

By the time she reached her office, her cell phone had chimed, indicating a text message. A quick glance revealed Jack's number on the caller ID.

:-) back at ya. Have a great idea. Tell you tonight.

* * *

Jack's great idea involved packing enough for the weekend, tossing it into the trunk of her car and heading out after lunch on Friday. He'd refused to reveal their destination, which only added to Maddie's monumental case of nerves. Once they'd left the Atlanta skyline behind them, she tried again.

"Can you give me a hint about where we're going?"

"That's right," he said. "You don't like surprises."

"I guess I had too many when I was a kid. My parents' idea of a surprise usually meant the custody order had been changed and I got to move. So yeah, I'm not real fond of the unknown."

"Don't worry. It won't be unknown for long."

His cavalier attitude irked her. She reclined her seat and settled back. Maybe she could sleep the trip away. Lord knows, she hadn't had much sleep all week.

Sleep, however, fell prey to worry and concern. Just what did Jack have planned? All they were supposed to do was have sex once, and they could have done that in Atlanta. Maybe the fact they'd never decided whose bedroom to use had fueled the idea of a road trip. Of course, Jack had selected their destination, so, by default, did that make it his bed?

An hour after leaving town, they left the main highway. After a series of turns and progressively bumpier roads that were sure to destroy the suspension on her car, they came to a stop where a sign pointed to Pleasant Junction one way and Cedar Gap the other. Jack turned the car toward the latter.

"Is this where the banjoes start dueling?" she asked sarcastically.

"The mayor of Pleasant Junction would be real upset to hear you say that," he commented dryly. "But the Cedar Gap boys would probably invite you to pick up a banjo and start to strum."

"Be still my heart," she drawled mockingly. "How much farther? Or is that a surprise too?"

"We're almost there."

They passed a sign that read "Pair-o-Dice" and turned into what appeared to be fenced property. Several hundred yards further, Maddie saw a small house with cedar siding, surrounded by towering hardwood trees.

"Is this your cabin?" Maddie asked, remembering an earlier conversation.

"No, I have to pick up the keys from Charlotte."

Charlotte? Did he have an old girlfriend in this area, and why did she have the keys to his cabin?

As he pulled the car closer to the house, the front door opened and an older woman emerged. Tall and thin, with snow-white hair, she walked toward the car.

Jack shoved the gear-shift into park and turned off the ignition. "Come on and I'll introduce you."

He angled out of his seat and strode toward the woman, his arms spread wide. She moved into his embrace and kissed him on the cheek.

"It's wonderful to see you again, Jack. It's been too long." The woman watched as Maddie exited and shielded her eyes from the afternoon sun. "And who is this lovely young lady?"

"This is my wife, Madelyn. Come here, honey."

The brief pause between *my* and *wife* wasn't lost on Maddie, but in all fairness, she had trouble referring to him as her husband. She could overlook it.

"Wife? Jack, you never even told me you were engaged. How long have you two been married? And why wasn't I invited to the wedding?"

"We've only been married for a week. It was a small ceremony. Just family. And we got married on the spur of the moment so..."

The woman's quick glance at Maddie's abdomen as she walked to Jack's side was obvious. Perhaps the elusive Charlotte was her daughter, and now Jack had showed up with a wife in tow.

Before Maddie could interject anything, the woman hugged her too. "Since Jack is being rude, I'll introduce myself. I'm Charlotte Tanner, and Jack is a dear friend. It's wonderful to meet you, Madelyn."

"Maddie. Please call me Maddie," she said awkwardly. So much for the girlfriend theory.

Charlotte reached into her pocket and produced a set of keys that she pressed into Jack's hand. "I'll let you two get on your way. I know you're in a hurry to get started on your honeymoon."

To her annoyance, Maddie found herself blushing.

"All the locks are new and keyed alike. The broken window has been replaced and the damage repaired. The security company got the alarm system installed and I had them set the code as you instructed. After you called Wednesday, I had my housekeeper spruce the place up and put a few things in the refrigerator for you. There's a casserole in there, too. All you have to do is put it in the microwave."

Jack pressed a kiss to the woman's cheek. "You're a gem, Charlotte. Don't know what I'd do without you."

"Well apparently you managed to get yourself married without me," she said, her sapphire blue eyes casting a look of mock censure in Jack's direction.

"I won't let it happen again." He winked at her.

Jack and Maddie said their good-byes and returned to the car. "What happened to your cabin?" she asked.

"Somebody broke the window in the back door and let themselves in. Nothing major, but I had a security system put in to deter future break-ins."

They rounded a bend and an unusual structure came into view. "Honey, we're home," Jack announced.

He pulled under a carport, killed the engine and popped the trunk. After hoisting a bag onto each shoulder, he walked to the back door as Maddie stood with her hands on her hips and scrutinized the dwelling. Or at least she thought it was a dwelling. Constructed of concrete block with chipped and faded white paint, the single-level building had no windows along the side visible from the approach. She could only imagine how gloomy the interior must be.

"Are you sure this is inhabitable? It doesn't look like a cabin to me."

"You can't judge things by the outside, Maddie," he said. "Lord knows, though, people have been doing it to me all my life."

"But it's a barn. I think."

"It *was* a barn. Come on and I'll show you what a little imagination and hard work can accomplish."

Jack twisted the new key then swung open the back door. He stepped inside, punched the alarm code into a keypad and then stepped back and motioned for Maddie to enter. He followed, dropped their bags on the tile floor in the entryway and went through the kitchen to the front windows to open the drapes.

Sunlight flooded the interior and Maddie gasped in surprise. What appeared to be an old, faded concrete block barn on the outside had been completely remodeled into a mountain getaway that invited guests to come in, kick off their shoes and stay a while.

The kitchen, while small, had granite countertops, stainless appliances and a pot rack hanging from the ceiling. The large gas range was a cook's dream come true. An eclectic mix of colorful pottery graced the countertops and the space between the tops of the cabinets and the nine-foot ceiling.

Slowly she moved into the living room and saw it also served as a dining area. The hardwood floors gleamed around the edges of two large area rugs, which served to define the living and dining areas. The room was furnished with comfortable upholstered pieces and a round claw-foot oak table and four chairs.

"These floors are beautiful, Jack."

"They're old hardwood. I recycled them from the house that was originally on this property. Part of it is in Charlotte's house, too."

"Did you build all this?" she asked, spreading her arms wide. "And Charlotte's house?"

"I'll tell you all about it later. Come on and let me show you the rest of the place."

He pulled her in front of a picture window with a postcard view of the surrounding area. "There's a covered deck across the front here and down one side. I love to sit out there with a cup of coffee first thing in the morning and just watch the day unfold."

"I can understand why. It's breathtaking."

Jack opened the front door and stepped out onto the deck, tugging Maddie behind him. "There's a hot tub on the side. The view's even better when you're up to your neck in hot water."

"I'll bet." Maddie stepped to the waist-high railing and studied the vista. She inhaled and her lungs filled with fresh air scented with the aroma of evergreen trees.

"Maybe we'll get to take it for a little test drive this weekend."

"Not until after…you know. All that hot water could thwart your…your swimmers."

Jack shook his head and laughed. "If I didn't know better, I'd think you married me only for my swimmers."

"I did," she stated flatly and returned to the house.

"I'd like to freshen up before dinner, she said over her shoulder. "Where's my room?"

Jack retrieved their bags from the kitchen then walked to the far side of the living area. Maddie followed him through a small hallway to a bedroom with the same postcard view of the mountains. A large iron bed dominated the room. The only other furnishings were a small rustic dresser and a nightstand and lamp. A patchwork quilt in earth tones covered the bed, and another was folded over the footboard.

Jack placed both their bags on the bed. "I'll show you around, not that there's much to see."

He opened the door that led from the bedroom to the deck and pointed out the hot tub. A pocket door separated the bedroom from the bathroom, which also opened to the hall. Then he opened a door at the far end of the hall and Maddie expected to find another bedroom.

"And this is the closet. Only one in the house other than the pantry. With space at a premium, I decided to do it this way. I mean, it's not like I live here all the time."

"You only have one bedroom," she stated flatly.

"I only need one bedroom. Where would I put a guest room anyway?"

"Don't you ever invite guests up here?"

Jack's eyes narrowed and his jaw clenched.

"Then where are you going to sleep?" A hint of panic colored her voice.

"Where do you think?"

"But where will I sleep?"

His lips tilted in a wicked grin. "Hey, we're on our honeymoon."

"Oh, no." Maddie backed away from him, looking like a cornered animal. "This isn't a honeymoon, and why did you tell that woman it was? My ovulation test was positive and you dragged me out of town up here to God knows where. I assumed we came up here so we could...and now you're talking about well, you know."

"Your accusations pierce me to the heart," he said mockingly. "Have I said anything about *you know*?"

"No, but that's what you expect."

"Now I'm really wounded. You're lumping me in with every moron you deal with in court."

"And you're assuming I'd get here and jump right in bed with you. It's just supposed to be a...a..."

"A one-night stand?"

She huffed out an impatient breath. "You make it sound so sleazy. And why didn't you tell me there was only one bedroom?"

She stormed back to the living room and flopped onto the couch.

"Easy there. Don't be so rough on my bed."

She sent him a puzzled look. "But you said..."

"I never said anything. You jumped to conclusions."

Jack sat beside her and nudged her with his shoulder. "Look at us. Already fighting on our honeymoon."

Maddie sneaked a sideways glance and couldn't contain her giggle. "Yeah, we're something, aren't we?" She patted him on the thigh then realized where her hand was and quickly pulled it back.

"Just like an old married couple," he said.

Not exactly.

* * *

After a cold shower and a shave, Jack tugged on jeans and a t-shirt and headed to the coffee pot. He had spent the past fifteen hours either walking on eggshells or lying sleepless on the sofa, fantasizing about the woman sleeping in the next room. He disarmed the security system and slipped onto the deck with a freshly brewed cup of liquid sunshine and settled into a chair.

This was Ovulation Day and time for them to have sex. He had tried to be sensitive to her feelings, but sometimes she was the most infuriating woman on the planet. He enjoyed their verbal sparring and tried not to let it go too far. But the thought of sex with her made him howling-at-the-moon crazy and that couldn't be good.

They'd discussed the sex thing. He understood it was one time only. He'd come to the cabin expecting to sleep on the couch. Yet she'd rushed to judgment and labeled him a jackass. He might be unreliable, undependable and irresponsible in some areas of his life, but there were two where he was not: his business and sex.

Having grown up with a single mother and an unknown father, Jack was unyielding about contraception. Until now, he'd been resolute in his determination not to bring another child into the world. And if it had meant wearing six condoms at one time, so be it.

Take care of her, Jack. Promise me.

He sipped his coffee and remembered how "take care of her" had evolved into "get her pregnant." At least he hadn't had to stop at a drugstore along the way for a box of condoms. He pushed against the floor, set the rocking chair into motion and laughed.

"What's so funny?"

He twisted and found Maddie standing in the doorway, her eyes still hooded from drowsiness and her hair mussed. She wore a tank top and pink sleep pants that were slung low on her hips and brushed her red toenails. She'd tossed a lightweight jacket around her shoulders to ward off the morning mountain chill, but Jack could see her nipples harden against the fabric of her top.

"Just thinking about something at work," he lied as his inner hound dog howled and his body reacted to her. His morning erection had only just dissipated before she'd appeared in the door.

She pulled the door shut and padded to the rocking chair beside him. "I've been thinking, too," she said as she lowered herself into the rocker beside his.

Here it comes.

Cancellation city. Termination time. *Coitus interruptus* before they'd even started.

"I think we should just go ahead and do it and get it over with." She tilted her head down and stared at her toes. Jack stared at them, too.

Do it.

The woman was going to have sex with a man who was virtually a stranger, so of course she couldn't speak in anything but euphemisms.

"If it's okay with you, that is."

She curled her toes against the decking and pulled the jacket tighter around her. All the while she refused to make eye contact with Jack, and she appeared as nervous as a virgin.

No way, he thought and banished the thought quickly.

"If it's not, we can wait until tonight."

She was ruining everything. He'd wanted to grill steaks and eat in front of the fireplace. Share a bottle of wine. Laugh and flirt and woo her so that when he finally took her to bed it seemed more like a seduction and less like a corporate negotiation.

"No, no. If you want to do it—to have sex now, we will." He'd said the word. He might not have removed the proverbial kid gloves, but he'd at least pulled them halfway off.

He watched as a blush ran across her face like a fever, and she worried her bottom lip with her teeth. He wanted to reach out and comfort her, reassure her that everything would be fine. He wished he could tell her that once would be enough and she wouldn't have to go through this awkward experience again.

However, his traitorous body wished differently, and he was primed and ready. Jack set his coffee mug beside the chair and stood. He reached for her hand and helped her up, and then he pulled her into his arms. He tucked her against his shoulder and breathed in the floral scent of her shampoo.

He heard her breath hitch, and he whispered assurances in her ear. He promised her their plan would work and wished he could promise her the moon and stars and more.

By the time they reached the bedroom, he had tugged off his t-shirt and his jeans felt a size too small. He'd left them unbuttoned, the only thing keeping them from causing permanent damage. He wanted them off as soon as possible, but would tolerate the discomfort to let Maddie take the lead.

She had left the covers folded down, which left him with nothing to do but watch her turn around and pull her top over her head before hooking her thumbs in the waistband of her sleep pants and lowering them past her hips. He watched her wiggle as she shimmied and let the pants puddle around her feet, and wished like hell he was the one undressing her. Under the severe business suits she normally wore was a body that should require a Surgeon General's warning: Smoking Hot Woman—could be dangerous to your health. And soon he'd have that body under him—warm, naked and willing.

Still facing away from him, she crawled onto the bed and pulled the sheet to her chin. Her cheeks remained flushed, and as she finally established eye contact with him, he reached for his zipper. Her gaze never wavered as he lowered it carefully and freed his erection.

He stripped off the jeans and crawled in next to her. Hesitantly he reached for the sheet and lowered it to her waist. She instinctively crossed one arm over her breasts and Jack slowly and tenderly nudged it away. He wanted to see her. To gauge how aroused she was. To figure out how he was going to have sex without making love.

"Don't be embarrassed," he whispered as he took her hand in his and gave it a reassuring squeeze.

"Easy for you to say," she replied as her eyes filled with tears. She blinked to no avail and they spilled over, creating damp paths down her face.

Jack propped on one elbow and brushed the tears away with his thumb. "Come here," he whispered, sliding his free hand around her waist and pulling her against him. She was definitely warm and naked, and if she'd just loosen up and let her body respond to his, she'd be willing as well.

Framing her face with his hand, he shifted and pressed a tender kiss first to her forehead and then to each eyelid. She tensed under his touch, and he repeated the kisses until she relaxed and sighed with contentment.

Tentatively, he skimmed a fingertip down her arm, testing her reaction, and when she remained relaxed, he took the next step. He cupped her breast in his hand, the flesh pliant under his fingers. With his thumb, he rubbed the nipple until it beaded under his touch.

"So beautiful," he murmured as his own body reacted further.

She reached for him and he savored the thrill of her touch. When she trailed her hand down his side and boldly circled his erection with her fingers, his back arched off the bed and he thrust into her grip.

His hand dipped between her legs, into the curls at the top of her thighs.

"You aren't ready," he said, his voice low and husky. He nuzzled at her neck and nipped her earlobe.

"I am," she insisted, twisting so her lower body made contact with his. She ground her pelvis against his, causing Jack to suck in a harsh breath. "Today's the day we have to do this and—"

Jack groaned in frustration. "That's not what I meant. You're not aroused. It'll be lots better if you are ready."

Maddie fell back against the pillow and Jack returned to her neck, licking at the fluttering pulse point there before kissing a trail past her breasts to her belly. Her muscles tightened then released for a moment before she inched away from him.

"There's a bottle of lubricant in my suitcase. Just get that."

"And get out of this comfortable bed? Natural is better, babe." Jack tucked a strand of hair behind her ear.

She gathered the sheet around her, breaking the mood. "Yeah, Mr. Food Additives and MSG. Like you'd know what natural was."

"I'm serious, babe—"

"Don't call me that. I'm not your babe. I'm just your…your…"

"Wife. You're just my wife who wanted to get pregnant, and that's what I'm trying to do. So fine. Whatever. I'll get the stuff, but it would be a lot more pleasurable if you were aroused."

"This isn't about pleasure," she said, pulling the sheet higher. "It's about making a baby. That's all."

The hell it was. He hooked two fingers under her chin and tilted her face upward. He surveyed her expression then rubbed his thumb over her bottom lip. "It's always about pleasure, Maddie. Sex without pleasure is failure. What this isn't about is hearts and forever. But there's no reason why both of us can't enjoy the baby-making process."

Her lips parted, but her gaze never wavered. He watched the muscles in her throat work as she swallowed, and when she made no attempt to agree with him, he played what he hoped was his trump card.

"You can't get what you want unless I get my pleasure. That's a given. But I'm not the selfish bastard most people think I am. I want you to get pleasure from this, too. And until I'm satisfied that you've enjoyed this, it goes no further."

Her eyes blazed with anger. "But that's…that's blackmail."

His finger traced a line from her chin to her navel, neatly bisecting her body. "Sweetheart, insisting that you enjoy this is not blackmail," he explained as he pressed his hand to her abdomen. "I like to call it the gentlemanly thing to do."

* * *

His argument was an excellent one, but Maddie still considered it blackmail. And did he have to look so good when he said it?

She thought she had clarified their arrangement. They had an agreement. For heaven's sake, they'd been married for a week and this morning was the first time he'd even seen her in her pajamas, much less been in bed with her. She'd been very careful to avoid anything that could be misinterpreted. Jack might be handsome as hell, and she might still have a healthy libido, but the twain couldn't meet.

"All I wanted was sperm, and I had it all planned. Then you waltzed into my house and flashed your smile and started questioning whether sperm donors were completely honest on their applications." She boiled with indignation, but tried to keep it under control, which was all but impossible lying naked beside Jack with his large, warm hand flat on her stomach. She didn't want to react to him, but her body wasn't obeying orders to remain unresponsive.

"If I hadn't listened to you, I'd probably be lying on my back in a fertility clinic right now with—"

"With a turkey baster between your legs. And once your ass-wipe of a judge found out what you'd done, half your case load would go down the toilet," he countered. "That's why we did what we did, wasn't it?" He broke physical contact and tucked the sheet around her.

Once again his argument was spot on. Every step of the way, the decision had been hers and hers alone. Every step of the way, she'd kept her emotions in check and her eye on her goal. Maddie had married Alex for love and for forever. He was safe. He was secure and faithful and dependable—everything her father had not been. Since she handled heated mediations, tense settlement conferences and bitter divorce trials for a living, she felt pretty certain that kind of marriage she had with Alex didn't come along more than once in a lifetime.

She was especially sure marriage to Jack wouldn't be the same.

He was different from Alex in almost every way. Despite the physical attraction, she would rather spend the rest of her life without a husband than risk another heartbreak like she had suffered when Alex died.

And she damn well wasn't going to risk a child's psychological well-being and security by becoming emotionally involved with Jack.

Selfish as it sounded, any child she had would be hers alone. There would be no repeat of the custody wars her parents had waged. Maddie had ensured that to the best of her ability with the heavily revised documents Jack agreed to sign.

Now she was just an arm's length away from the goal and she was quibbling over an orgasm. Most women would trade places with her in a heartbeat. Blackmail or not, Jack was going to stand his ground, and if she wanted to get pregnant, then she'd have to play by his rules.

If only his rules didn't make her feel so guilty. If only the sight of his nakedness didn't make her feel so…ready.

"I'm going to go get another cup of coffee and then see if there's a tree that needs to be chopped down or a fence that needs mending." He scrubbed a hand across his jaw, which was clenched tightly. He rolled off the bed and stood, unashamed of his nakedness. Grabbing the clothing he'd tossed beside the bed, he moved toward the door.

"Don't go." Her words were little more than a whisper. "I'll do it your way. I'll play by your rules."

Jack turned slowly, obviously irritated and even more obviously no longer aroused. "This isn't about rules or about *my* way or *your* way. I just don't know how to do it—how to make love to a woman—any *other* way."

Maddie's eyes were glassy with tears. She didn't want to beg, but she feared if he left now, Jack would end up on the couch and Ovulation Day would go uncelebrated. He began to turn his shirt right-side out.

Don't let him get away, her mind screamed.

She held out her hand and took a deep breath. "Can we try this again?"

The corner of his eye twitched and his lips flattened into a line. Definitely not the signs of a man willing to take a second chance.

"Or later would be fine, too," she murmured.

Embarrassed, she turned and stretched for the robe she'd left lying across the foot of the bed, but before she could reach it, the mattress dipped and Jack was behind her, pulling her body to his. Her curves molded to the outline of his muscular body, and his breath tickled the back of her neck. Relief flooded her and she released the breath she hadn't realized she'd been holding in.

He hadn't left.

She wiggled back against him and savored the sensation of him growing hard against her. With her encouragement—verbal and nonverbal—he took his time, molding her breasts with his hands, circling her navel with his tongue; touching and kissing her absolutely everywhere until she was dizzy from the fury of her climax.

When he rose over her and settled between her legs, her body opened to the insistent nudging from his erection. Her breath caught in sweet anguish as he pressed into her, and once her body had accommodated him, she began to rock her hips, slowly at first and then more frantically.

He matched her rhythm, his biceps bunching as he held his weight off her, sweat beading on his forehead as he thrust in and out of her wetness.

When he suddenly stopped and pulled back, she cried out and wrapped one leg around his to hold him to her.

"Wait," he gasped, resting his forehead against hers. "Slow down."

She grabbed his buttocks and arched, missing the fullness of him, wanting him all the way back inside her.

He released an agonizing groan and straightened his arms, almost withdrawing from her. "It's too fast." His voice was ragged.

Desperate. "It's the first time I've…" He closed his eyes in concentration.

"I doubt that," she shot back incredulously.

"It's the first time I've ever had sex without a condom, and if we don't slow down, it's going to be over before it starts."

The enormity of Jack's statement—and his confession—was both endearing and empowering. She was privy to something she doubted Jack had revealed to another woman. And with that bit of information, her opinion of Jack Worth shifted.

She lay still beneath him, giving him full control, and when he pushed back inside her and began to thrust again with a steady rhythm, it was with a passion she'd never expected from him. When he sat back on his thighs and his grip on her hips tightened, she responded powerfully and bunched the sheets in her fists.

When it hit, the pleasure was explosive. Her breath caught in her throat as another furious orgasm blazed through her. She arched again, tightening around him, squeezing until he drove in one last time and she felt the power of his climax ripple through him.

"Maddie," he murmured as he collapsed against her, then gathered her in his arms and rolled to his side to take his weight off her.

"I…it…" Words eluded her, and what could she say anyway that wouldn't sound trite or clichéd? Thanking him seemed unnecessary and even insulting. Telling him he'd been right about the pleasure part might give him the wrong idea.

"Yeah, I know," he whispered against her ear.

Jack brushed his lips tenderly against hers, then released her from his embrace and sat up. "Here," he said, grabbing a pillow and sliding it under her hips. "You need to lie still and let things work."

He pulled the sheet over her before heading to the bathroom. Maddie heard the toilet flush, then the sound of running water. When Jack reappeared, he had a towel tied around his hips.

"Can I get you anything? You didn't have breakfast so you must be starving. I'll bring you something to eat."

He flung off the towel, giving her another view of his perfect behind, and searched for his jeans. He pulled them on as he padded to the door. After glancing back at her once more, he left her alone.

No matter how breathtaking sex with Jack had been, no matter that he'd made her come twice, it was still only sex; nothing more than the transfer of seminal fluid from one body to another for the express purpose of conceiving a child.

And if she believed that, she would need more than a contract and a promise to protect her from the real possibility of falling for Jack Worth.

Seven

Maddie shoved aside the breakfast tray after nearly inhaling the food Jack had prepared. She tugged the sash of her robe tighter around her waist.

Her waist.

In a few months she might not have a waist.

Her hand splayed across her abdomen and she wondered if their attempt had been successful. Could conception be happening now? Would she be pregnant by nightfall but unable to know for another few weeks?

Tears blurred her vision, and she blinked in an effort to hold them in check. She had expected to be awash with emotions after she and Jack had sex, but what she sensed right now went far beyond her expectations.

Why had sex with him left her such an emotional mess? Jack had driven her to heights she hadn't imagined. And after bringing her the breakfast tray, he had disappeared into the bathroom again to finish dressing and shave.

He stepped into the bedroom doorway. "I need to go to Charlotte's and check on a few things," he said. "Will you be okay here by yourself?"

Maddie nodded. "Will you have your cell phone just in case I need you?" She snagged a small bit of crisp bacon from her plate and popped it into her mouth.

"Yeah. I'm not sure how much she has on her to-do list, so I have no idea how long I'll be gone."

"You go take care of…whatever," she said with a wave of her hand. "I'll be fine."

Jack turned to move away.

"The breakfast was delicious, by the way," Maddie added, almost as an afterthought. "Do you treat all your women to breakfast in bed?"

As soon as the words left her mouth she regretted the callous comment. She was jumping to conclusions again, judging the man by rumors from sources she now realized were most likely unreliable.

"Only my wives," he retorted, a momentary spark of displeasure flashing across his face. "And just in case you're wondering, you are the first."

His steps were heavy as he crossed the cabin, and only after she heard the door close did she carry her tray to the kitchen.

After washing the dishes and set them in the drainer to dry, she returned to the bedroom and pulled clean clothes from her bag. She showered, dressed and combed her wet hair into place, allowing it to air dry. Pulling out the paperback novel she'd brought along, she settled into one of the upholstered recliners to read.

The mystery couldn't hold her attention for long, and her thoughts wandered to Jack's departure. What was the story behind him and Charlotte? He'd promised to explain, and she needed to remember to ask. If she'd been family, he probably would have introduced her as such. As it stood, the elderly woman was just another missing piece of the puzzle Jack has become.

Did he really have to play handyman, or was he simply giving her space because he knew things would be awkward between them after sex? Once again she rested her hand across her belly and said a silent prayer that this attempt had succeeded. Because as amazing as the physical aspect had been, Maddie wasn't sure she could withstand the emotional onslaught of having sex with Jack again.

She wondered if much of her reaction was because it had been such a long time since she'd been with anyone sexually. Alex had been dead a year and was sick for two years before that. Chemo had left him impotent. When your husband was fighting for his life, sex wasn't exactly on the top of the priority list.

And now sex—sex with Jack—had become a priority, and despite all the talks she'd given herself in the bathroom mirror, she still experienced a certain degree of completely unrealistic guilt. Perhaps it stemmed from her own relative inexperience with men. Jack was only her second lover. She'd never trusted men because of her father's infidelity, and her stepfather had only increased her distrust.

Alex had been her safe haven, her security, and now he was gone, and in his place stood a man who'd made her feel alive again. Maddie thought back to Jack's insistence that their coupling involve pleasure. And he had undeniably delivered on that issue. No doubt about it, Jack Worth knew how to satisfy a woman.

Jack wasn't just a good lover. He was a great lover. He was her best lover, and if a pregnancy test in two weeks showed a positive result, she'd never get to experience her best lover again. Why did that thought rock her to her soul? Theirs wasn't a love affair to last for all time; it was a marriage purely for convenience. Sex once, hopefully a pregnancy and then they could resume their separate lives under the same roof. And that was beginning to scare her because she might just be wanting more from their arrangement.

* * *

Maddie woke on Sunday to a quiet house and wondered if Jack was still asleep on the sofa or if he'd escaped to Charlotte's again. He had disappeared for most of Saturday afternoon and returned in time to throw two steaks on the grill and feed her dinner. From the array of convenience food wrappers she'd seen in the trash bin at home, she had assumed he didn't know how to cook. Here was another surprise.

Pulling on her robe, she tiptoed to the kitchen. Jack lay still on the sofa, partially covered by a blanket and snoring softly. She tugged one corner of the fleece material and covered his bare feet. He turned his head, muttered something and settled back into whatever—or whomever—he was dreaming about. She'd insisted on separate bedrooms and only having sex when she was fertile. So why was her mind filling with thoughts of being cradled all night in his arms?

As quietly as possible, she pulled a package of pastries from the freezer and put them in the microwave to heat. Then she filled the coffee maker with water and scooped grounds into the basket. As the machine gurgled and hissed, she tiptoed back to the bathroom. After brushing her teeth and fixing her hair, she applied a little mascara and lip-gloss and dressed in the slacks and blouse she planned to wear back to Atlanta later that afternoon.

As she walked from the bedroom, head bent to fasten the bottom button of her blouse, she collided with a solid wall of bare chest. Jack wrapped his arms around her to steady her and when she looked up at his face, that zing traveled through her again and settled in her belly. Jack's sleep pants rode low on his hips, revealing a tanned and sculpted body—sculpted not from hours in a gym, but hours of hard work. A day's growth of beard darkened his jaw and sleep still clouded his eyes.

"Sorry," he mumbled, releasing his hold on her and shuffling past her into the bathroom.

The sizzle disappeared. Probably just hunger, she thought, praying her body didn't betray her by turning her face and neck bright crimson.

She returned to the kitchen, removed the pastries from the microwave and poured herself a cup of coffee. She needed the caffeine to drive away the lingering sleepiness brought on by alternating dreams of making love to Jack under the stars and cradling her baby in her arms. And as quickly as she'd taken the first sip of coffee, she remembered that pregnant women shouldn't consume caffeine.

Jack walked into the kitchen just as she dumped the entire cup down the sink. "You should have nuked it if it was too cold. That's what I do," he said, grabbing a mug from the cupboard and poured himself a cup.

"It's not that," she said hesitantly. "It's just that if I got pregnant yesterday, I shouldn't be having caffeine."

His gaze slipped to her abdomen, and the blush she'd avoided earlier colored her cheeks. To his credit he said nothing and snagged a pastry from the plate.

"You probably shouldn't be having this either," he added, holding out the sugary confection. "I guess I should be making sure you eat right and not filling the fridge with junk food." He scarfed it down in three bites then grabbed another. "We should leave here by three to avoid the Sunday afternoon rush back into town. And if you'd like the grand tour of Pleasant Junction and Cedar Gap, we need to leave a little earlier."

"Maybe next time?"

"Gotcha," he replied, a bemused grin curling his lips.

If there was a next time.

* * *

"What's this?" Jack asked, holding up an engraved invitation. "Did we get invited to some fancy-ass wing-ding?" He turned the envelope over to check the address.

Maddie snatched it from him. "The *fancy-ass wing-ding* is the annual charity gala for the Atlanta Women's League. They raise money for abused and neglected children, but we're not going. I returned the RSVP card week before last."

Jack breathed out a sigh of relief. "Good, cause I'm just all gala-ed out. And besides, I have nothing to wear to a fancy-ass wing-ding."

Maddie shook her head and returned to unloading the groceries she'd picked up on the way home from work. In the ten days since they'd been at the cabin, Jack had been spending less time sprawled on the couch downstairs watching sports and more time upstairs making sure she ate properly and helping out with small things.

"I guess you get invited to things like this because of your work?" He vaguely remembered Alex mentioning some sort of deal where he had to wear a tux and make small talk all night. Jack was more of a cowboy boots, jeans and sports talk kind of guy, and he was secretly glad Maddie had declined the invitation.

"Yes, and Judge Benson's wife is the president of the Women's League, too. We've served on a couple of boards together. Normally I'd have gone to Fire and Ice but I just didn't want to face Judge Ward because I know he'll be there too. His wife—"

"Judge Ward? The one you want to convince that you're happily married?"

"Yes," she said, drawing the word out until it contained more than one syllable.

"Could you call them back and tell them you changed your mind?"

A plan was forming in his mind. A plan that if properly executed should convince even the cynical Judge Ward that he and Maddie were madly in love and destined for a long and happy life together. Jack abhorred deception, especially since he'd been the victim of his mother's. But sometimes a little white lie made things better and no one was worse for its commission.

"I suppose," she began hesitantly. "But I can see the wheels turning in your head and I don't think I'm going to like the result."

"Hear me out, Maddie." He pulled out a chair from the kitchen table, turned it around and sat, resting his arms along the back of the chair. "The big reason we said *I do* is because of Judge Ward and what he'd do if you got pregnant and you weren't married. And Tess even told me that we needed to make sure that as far as the public was concerned we *were* married. She said I should take you out—to dinner, to a play or the symphony. You know, go places where we'd be seen, especially by the people who really count."

"When did Tess tell you that?"

"Right after she promised to castrate me with a dull paring knife if I did anything to hurt you."

"And she would, too."

Jack flinched. How two decidedly different women could be such good friends still baffled him. Or maybe Maddie had a sadistic streak she kept well hidden.

"Anyway, my uh…body parts notwithstanding, that charity deal would be the perfect place to be seen. We can dance, schmooze and drink their liquor, and I promise you I'll be the most impressive husband there."

"I don't know, Jack. I'm not sure we could pull it off." Maddie eyed him warily.

"Oh, ye of little faith. Are you afraid you can't do it? He stood and strode toward her. "Or are you afraid *I* can't?"

He'd been doubted most of his life, and until Alex Prescott had taken a chance on him, Jack had doubted himself. Now he was ready to rise to another trial, no matter what.

"You'll have to get a tuxedo," she said in a challenging manner.

Jack groaned inwardly at the thought of dressing in a penguin suit. "How do you know I don't already have one?" He lobbed the verbal ball back into her court and waited for her answer.

Maddie folded the last paper bag from the grocery store, and Jack could tell she was working through her answer. Thinking ahead to anticipate his next question. Formulating several alternative replies, just like she'd do in a courtroom.

"I guess I don't," she responded.

"Well, I don't." He moved closer until they were standing on opposite sides of the kitchen island. "If you were to change your mind and decide to go, I'd have to rent one. I could get Millie to help me." He remembered the dent the Armani tie had made in his checkbook and reconsidered. "Or you could help me. Then if anyone asked, you could say you helped me pick it out."

Maddie gave him a look of disbelief.

"Okay, I'm reaching. But it can work, Maddie. I know it can. Are you in?" He leaned against the island until the edge of the granite top bit into his hip. "Will you go out with me on…?" He picked up the invitation again to verify the date. "Friday night?"

When she nodded in agreement, he pumped his fist then resumed a more composed demeanor. "I guess the question now is do *you* have something to wear? Or am I going to have to help you shop for a dress?"

"I can hear the sarcasm just dripping from your voice, Jack. You can relax. I have a black dress I've worn to a few other events and it will work just perfectly."

"Black? But this is the Fire and Ice ball. You need to be wearing red because…" Jack cut himself off before he told her she was red hot and sexy and he embarrassed himself.

"Because?"

"Well, because it's Fire and Ice and a red dress would be real fiery. How about we meet at the mall tomorrow after work and find you a hot red dress and get me fitted for a tux?"

Maddie turned back to the refrigerator and opened the freezer compartment. "Do you want healthy frozen pizza for dinner or healthy frozen lasagna?"

She was avoiding him. But why? Didn't most women love to shop, especially when someone else was picking up the tab? Or had he told her the shopping trip was on him? Regardless, her avoidance bothered him.

He stepped around the island and moved beside her to stare into the freezer. "Give me the pizza and then tell me why you changed the subject." He pulled two boxes from the freezer, opened them and handed them off to Maddie for microwaving.

"I just have a lot on my mind right now."

"Anything I can help with?" He turned her around to face away from him, then placed his hands on her shoulders and began to knead the knotted muscles in her shoulders.

"You already did. Weekend before last."

Jack calculated mentally and realized that Maddie should find out soon if she'd gotten pregnant. This time next week she could be picking out baby furniture and interviewing nanny candidates. He'd help with anything he could—or more accurately, what Maddie would allow. She'd been adamant she would make it on her own.

Her baby would have a mother and a sperm donor—pretty much like what Jack's life had been, but this baby's donor would have a name.

"Yeah, I guess I did." He continued kneading and recognized the moment she began to relax. "How soon will you be able to tell for sure?"

"Probably on Saturday, but sometimes when I've been under a lot of stress I can be a day or two late."

"Have you bought one of those home tests yet? It should tell you how long you have to wait."

"I got one at the grocery store today. I…uh…left it in the car."

He'd seen the woman stark naked and yet she was timid about a home pregnancy test? Of course, part of him could understand. He hated to buy condoms from a female store clerk, especially one old enough to be his mother or grandmother. He always wondered if they were secretly damning him to hell for having sex so much he needed the super-size box.

"Get it and I'll take care of the microwave. Then we'll figure out what to do." He gave her a little push toward the garage, then pulled two forks from the drawer and poured two glasses of decaf iced tea. By the time she'd returned with a small blue box, he'd placed their dinner on the kitchen table and made a resolution that regardless of what Maddie thought she wanted, he'd see to it that the baby—if there was one—wouldn't be called a bastard.

* * *

By noon the following day, Jack had a pair of shiny shoes and a black tuxedo and hanging on his closet door, but he'd drawn the line at a bow tie. Instead he chose a regular necktie, solid black with subtle black stripes. He'd also drawn the line at a frilly shirt and picked a plain white one. Selecting his tuxedo had been the easy part of the shopping trip.

He met Maddie after work at the same mall where Millie had taken him shopping, and when he saw the look of approval on her face, he made a mental note to send Millie a dozen roses. Two dozen if the mission succeeded.

Where his noontime shopping trip had been quick and easy, finding the perfect dress for Maddie got off to a slow start. Millie had warned him he would be spending lots of time sitting on chairs outside dressing rooms, offering opinions that often didn't amount to anything and then escorting her to the next store to repeat the process.

At the fifth or sixth store, just when she seemed ready to surrender tearfully, a twenty-something sales clerk disappeared into a back room and returned with another dress. "Someone asked us yesterday afternoon to hold this, but she hasn't come back. It's been more than twenty-four hours so you can try it if you like."

In the past Jack had heard women talk about not knowing what you wanted until you saw it, and he immediately saw that principle in action. Maddie's eyes brightened as she followed the clerk into the dressing room area and he sat in yet another uncomfortable chair and waited, calling upon the name of every deity he could remember, willing them to make the dress fit.

When Maddie emerged from the dressing room, Jack's prayers had been answered. She wore a red, strapless, floor-length dress with a silvery-white pattern scattered throughout. Red trim crisscrossed at the top and accentuated her breasts while the fabric was gathered at the waist and made her appear even curvier.

She stepped in front of a long mirror and turned slowly, taking in her reflection from all angles.

"The ruching at the waist looks perfect on you," the young woman commented. "You have the perfect figure for it." She adjusted the back and hem, and then stepped back to scrutinize her handiwork. "Don't you think the dress looks fabulous on your wife?"

She had directed the question to Jack, but he was so mesmerized he could hardly think, much less answer.

Maddie turned back to face the mirror and frowned. "If you don't think it's right, we can try another—"

"It's perfect. Absolutely perfect," Jack said, snapping out of his trance. "It's fire and ice and I don't think you could find anything better if we looked forever."

"You aren't just saying that because your feet hurt or you're hungry, are you?" Jack heard the frustration in her voice.

He rose from the chair and moved to stand behind her. He placed his hands on her shoulders then skimmed his palms lightly down her arms and back up again. "My feet are just fine, thank you," he whispered in her ear. His gaze captured hers in the mirror and the only hunger he had was a longing for her. "This is the one, Maddie."

He traced one finger along the neckline of the dress to where it dipped between her breasts and she shivered beneath his touch.

"If you don't already have shoes, they have a fab pair of red sandals downstairs," the saleswoman piped in. "And of course you need to wear a diamond necklace and earrings. Tiffany is just half a mile up Peachtree Road."

Maddie swiveled to her right. "Of course," she said in agreement. "I'll check the shoe department."

The spell had been broken and the connection Jack had felt with his wife was gone. Maddie returned to the dressing room in a rustle of fabric, and he returned to his chair, wondering if the shoe department had more comfortable seats and if Tiffany sold anything with a price tag under the gross national product of a small country.

* * *

Jack paced the length of the family room and waited for Maddie to finish dressing. They had plenty of time to drive to the St. Germaine, park and make their properly timed entrance at the Fire and Ice ball. That is if they walked out the front door within the next twenty minutes.

Shower, shave, comb, put on a tux and tie the tie. It took thirty minutes tops. Jack reined in his impatience, though, not only because he knew Maddie wanted to make a good impression, but also because he suspected she was going to look like a million dollars and *he* got the first look.

He also reined in his libido because this wasn't about him; it was all about her and putting forth the right image. They'd have to smile, touch and act like they were in love. Jack found it difficult to deliberately deceive friends. Millie knew everything and so did Maddie's friend Tess. But everyone else had to believe they were crazy in love.

Jack was afraid, though, that after they behaved like a married couple in public until midnight, he'd want to behave like one in private until dawn.

He heard a cough from the opposite side of the room and turned. Maddie had looked gorgeous in the store. Now she was stunning except for...

"Why are you wearing pearls?" he asked, looking at her intently, seeing the same pearl necklace and earrings she'd worn at their wedding. "You told me you had diamonds."

She glanced away as if embarrassed.

"Alex gave them to me for our anniversary. I only wore them twice—at his funeral and…"

"And?" He raised an eyebrow a fraction of an inch.

"I guess we should be going now, hmmm?" She gathered her purse and wrap from the sofa and moved past him toward the garage.

He grasped her hand with enough force to stop her. "Why, Maddie? Why won't you wear them?" he asked.

She stiffened and raised her chin, sending him a defiant look. "The other time I wore them was the night he gave them to me. I wore them to bed. The diamonds and nothing else."

A mental picture of Maddie in bed, warm, wet and wearing nothing but diamonds had his blood doing a quick U-turn and heading south.

Unconsciously, he gripped her arm a little tighter and then heard her sharp intake of breath. He loosened his hold then rubbed his thumb along her delicate wrist.

"Wear them."

"But—"

"These are nice," he said, fingering the pearls around her neck. "But diamonds will be the ice to compliment the fire in your dress."

And maybe they'd be the ice to douse the fire in his groin.

"And what if someone asks me about them? How do I tell them they were a gift from my husband?"

"You tell them they *were* a gift from your husband. They don't need to know *which* husband."

"But—"

"Please? For me?"

He was a damn fool. His libido did not need any more goading, but he wanted Judge Thomas Jefferson Ward to leave the ball knowing without any doubt that Maddie was legally married and living in wedded bliss.

Maddie sighed, then pressed her purse and shawl into his hands and disappeared into her bedroom. She returned carrying a navy velvet jewelry box and a lighter blue pouch. Jack recognized the pouch from Tiffany and suspected the navy box bore their name, too.

He thought he'd done well purchasing her engagement ring from the exclusive shop, but he was afraid after he saw the contents of the box, he'd be demoted to the lightweight division.

Maddie opened the box and a diamond necklace contrasted starkly against the dark lining. Diamonds set in an X pattern were placed at intervals with round stones to create the look of a dazzling string of stars.

"Would you help me put it on? I have trouble with the clasp." She wrapped the necklace around her neck then turned her back to him.

Jack stepped forward and grasped the ends of the necklace, fumbling momentarily before securing them together. He let his hands slide from the back of her neck to her shoulders. The warmth of her skin seeped into his fingers, and unconsciously he gently kneaded her flesh.

He heard Maddie's breath catch in her throat and he removed his hands. He stepped back and Maddie turned around, fingering the necklace to straighten it. She picked up the blue pouch and shook it. A pair of earrings in the same star design fell into her palm. Skillfully she pulled off the backing and fastened the earring to her earlobe. Then she repeated the process with the other earring while Jack stood transfixed.

She'd been stunning before; now she was breathtaking. Jack felt the same way he had at Primrose Cottage—overwhelmed by her beauty and still not quite believing she'd agreed to his offer. And within a few days, they'd know whether their attempt at pregnancy had worked. If it had, he'd play things by ear and be as supportive as possible. If not, maybe she'd wear the diamonds in bed for him the next time they tried.

* * *

Jack braked the car in front of the hotel and angled out when the valet opened his door. He tossed the key to the young man and hurried to the other side to help Maddie maneuver her long skirt out of the car.

The St. Germaine was a remnant of the roaring twenties and had been renovated to its former glory a decade before. When they stepped into the San Regis ballroom, Jack cast a brief glance around the room. He'd come a long way from the trailer park on the south side of town.

Tables covered in white linen circled the perimeter. A half dozen small candles flickered on every table and the crystal chandeliers shimmered overhead to create a festive atmosphere.

Maddie was greeted immediately by several well-heeled older women and he was introduced to a bevy of Atlanta's upper crust.

"Would you like something to drink?" he asked Maddie, leaning close to be heard over the orchestra and several hundred voices echoing off the high ceilings. She smiled and nodded.

He left her in conversation with her boss's wife and made his way across the ballroom to the bar. He ordered scotch for himself and club soda for Maddie, and waited for the bartender to prepare the drinks. Two gray-haired men stepped beside him and both ordered bourbon.

"It looks like I'll probably get the party nod for the next election," one said in a deep southern drawl. "And when I win, I'm goin' to clean house in the ad litem program. I got one little gal who thinks she's pulled a fast one on me. But I have her number and I will not let someone who makes a joke of the institution of marriage represent helpless children in court."

"Good for you," his friend replied in an accent that indicated he'd been transplanted to Georgia. "Some of these young folks have no sense of decency any more, and it pains me to see them representing the laws of this state."

Jack dropped a few bills in the tip bowl and took two glasses from the bartender. He was sure the drawl belonged to Maddie's nemesis and hurried back to warn her.

"You'll never guess who I ran into at the bar," he said, pressing the tumbler into her hand. "Your old friend Judge Ward. Or at least I think it was from the way he was talking. I had to stifle the urge to deck him right there. I didn't think you would appreciate me killing a sitting judge at a charity ball. The papers would have a field day with that."

"Speaking of the devil," she mumbled, plastering a smile on her face. "Judge Ward, it's nice to see you again," she said, holding out her right hand. "And Mrs. Ward."

"Miz Prescott," he drawled, lifting her hand to his lips for a brief, and very affected, kiss. "Or are you using your married name?

So many of you younger gals don't change your names anymore. I suppose this is the brand-new husband I've been hearing about?" The man turned and extended his hand to Jack.

Jack introduced himself and tried to size up the man. He was probably more a legend in his own mind than a legend in his field, but he did wield the power to affect Maddie's career, and that's why Jack maintained an even composure. Knocking back the whole glass of scotch probably wasn't a good idea, so he handed it off to a passing waiter and eliminated the temptation.

"That's a beautiful ring," Mrs. Ward commented. "How long have you two been married, dear?"

"Just a few weeks now, isn't it?" the judge interrupted. "And it seems just like yesterday that your first husband passed. I was awfully sorry to hear about that. He was such a successful businessman and a real asset to this community." He surveyed Jack from his fresh haircut to the laces of his shiny shoes and flashed a smile as phony as Monopoly money.

Jack wanted to tell the man to take his innuendo and snobbery and stuff it, but for Maddie's sake he'd play nice.

"And what do you do for a living, Mr. Worth?" Mrs. Ward asked. Her interest seemed sincere.

"I'm in residential construction, ma'am. I've built homes for several football and baseball players here in the Atlanta area, and right now I'm working on a project for the owner of LRL Media Group."

"You're building Leland and Rosemarie Levernier's new house? Rosemarie showed me the blueprints and the interior designer's plans. It's going to be a lovely home. She was quite excited about it. I'll have to tell her I met her builder."

Jack smiled weakly and wondered just how much worse his luck could run tonight.

"You were partners with your wife's late husband weren't you?"

Your luck just ran out, man.

"Yes, sir. We were partners for seven years before he died."

"And wasn't it nice of you to take over the business and then marry your partner's widow so soon after his death?"

"With all due respect, sir, I'd love to stay here and chat with you and Mrs. Ward," Jack began, taking Maddie's hand in his. "But I need to dance with my wife because the orchestra just started playing our song."

Jack placed his right hand against Maddie's back and guided her toward the polished wood dance floor. He pulled her toward him and let his hand slide further down her back.

"I didn't know we had a song," she whispered. "Especially not 'Midnight Train to Georgia.'"

"We do now, and if we're going to convince the good judge, and I use the term quite loosely, you can't dance with me at arm's length." Jack tugged her closer and began to move to the music. "Relax." He put his lips next to her ear and spoke in a low tone. "We're supposed to look like we're dancing, not engaged in hand-to-hand combat. I suppose we should have practiced a little at home, huh?"

Maddie giggled and went from edgy to relaxed in two beats. She settled into his arms and matched his movement as the orchestra segued from one number to the next. Her breasts pressed against him and he breathed in her subtle perfume.

"I think we'll be okay if we just sway to the music, and I'll do my best to avoid stepping on those new shoes," he grinned.

"I always wanted to learn ballroom dancing. It was one of those things Alex and I never got around to." Jack caught a hint of melancholy in her voice.

If he closed his eyes, he could imagine Maddie in bed with him again, doing a different kind of dance. Jack began to hope against hope they hadn't studied well enough for the upcoming pregnancy test and failed so he could make love to her again. He ached to feel her touch against his bare skin, to hear her moan and feel her tremble as she came apart in his arms.

He pressed his lips to her temple then kissed down her cheek. He hesitated briefly before slanting his mouth across hers and brushing his lips gently against the velvet warmth of hers. Her lips parted and he tentatively touched his tongue to hers. Maddie breathed out on a sigh and kissed with a hunger that was at odds with her calm exterior.

The kiss sent a spiral of need straight to Jack's groin, making him the one who was stiff and edgy. He broke the kiss and opened his eyes. Her eyes fluttered open, then closed again as her hand moved to his neck and her fingers ruffled the hair at his nape.

Jack's lips descended to recapture hers. He sipped gently then nibbled greedily until she opened to him again and his tongue swept inside. Though it was feverish, the kiss had a dream-like intimacy that made him forget they were surrounded by hundreds of people. Made him forget this woman was his wife in name only. Made him forget that his life—their lives—might change drastically over the next few days.

The intimacy of their kiss was shattered, however, when someone nearby called out. "Get a room, you two."

Maddie startled and pulled away from the embrace.

"Stay close, sweetheart, or I'll embarrass us both even more," he muttered as he willed his blood supply to redirect itself back to his brain and furnish his gray matter with enough nourishment to figure out how to get himself and Maddie out of this situation.

A man could lie about a lot of things, but he couldn't fake a hard-on. Jack was definitely turned on and all it had required was a slow dance and a kiss. He felt as awkward as a twelve-year-old boy at his first dance, yet as excited as a teenager with his first girlie magazine.

He was with the prettiest girl in school and he wanted nothing more than to get a room and do all the wondrous things his traitorous mind imagined.

Eight

Jack punched the redial button on his cell phone and got the answering machine—again. He'd already left two messages on it as well as two on Maddie's cell phone.

Earlier in the afternoon when he'd joined some of his crew for an impromptu poker game, she had said nothing about leaving the house, but he knew how plans could change at the drop of a hat—or a phone call from Tess.

The ride home after the Fire and Ice ball had matched the theme of the event—a fiery sensation gnawing a hole in his gut and an icy reaction from Maddie when he tried to talk about what had happened between them.

Hell, she was probably shocked rather than giving him the cold shoulder. How many men ever wanted to talk about anything? That alone could get him an appearance on any of the afternoon talk shows.

Pulling his truck into the drive, he pressed the garage door remote and the door slipped open. His pulse kicked up a notch when he saw Maddie's car still parked in its usual spot in the left bay. He tamped down what was probably an overreaction. Seemed he'd been doing a lot of that lately.

Tess had probably swung by in her little red two-seater sports car and kidnapped Maddie for a Sunday matinee chick flick and dinner at some trendy bistro that served tofu and bean sprouts. Or perhaps Tess was getting an earful about the hard-on he had ground into her during their kiss—a kiss she'd been mighty damned involved in herself if memory served him correctly.

He let himself into the house and pocketed his keys. Grabbing a beer from the fridge, he reached for the light switch and froze when he spotted Maddie's purse and keys on the kitchen table.

She was avoiding him or she was asleep or… He shoved the negative thoughts from his mind. Treading lightly, he moved from the kitchen to the family room doorway. The low afternoon sun cast long shadows across the room—shadows that hid a lot.

He tilted his head, listening for any sound out of the ordinary, and then heard it—a sob, a sniffle, another sob.

Jack followed the sounds and found Maddie huddled under a blanket at the end of the sofa. "Maddie, honey, are you okay? Why didn't you pick up the phone or return my calls? I was worried."

She glanced up at him, her cheeks stained with tears and mascara smudged around both eyes. Curled up in the corner of the sofa, her legs pulled up and her chin propped on her knees, she seemed frail and weak—not at all the strong woman he knew her to be.

Jack knelt and put himself at eye level. "Tell me, please. What's the matter? Is there something I can do?"

Or was it something I did?

She shook her head and sniffled again. "It didn't work."

Didn't work? What didn't work? Then he squeezed his eyes shut and mentally cursed himself. He should have remembered this was *the* weekend and stayed home to be with her.

"Did you do more than one test?"

"No. I didn't need to use the test. I started this afternoon."

Jack scooped her into his arms and sat with her in his lap. He brushed her tears away, threading his fingers through the hair that clung to her damp cheek. He made shushing noises and rocked her back and forth like the baby she desperately wanted.

"It'll be okay, sweetheart," he crooned. "It'll be okay."

"It didn't work," she repeated. "I did everything right and it didn't work." Her disappointment was palpable, and Jack wasn't sure he could say anything that would soothe her and take away the sting of failure.

Maddie would make a wonderful mother. He was sure of it. She and her baby would be a wonderful family of two. Jack had spent hours as a child daydreaming about what it would be like to be part of a real family—mother, father, two-point-five kids, a dog and a house in the suburbs. He had given up that dream at a far too early age and settled for short-term, no-strings encounters, leaving a relationship as soon as it took a turn toward serious. Many women thought they could domesticate Jack Worth, but he always walked away.

None had been able to get him down the aisle until now, and the only reason for the ring on his left hand was that Jack Worth kept his promises. He had never seen the institution of marriage at work. His father had apparently bailed before his mother even knew she was pregnant. Connie Worth was simply one more notch on his bedpost.

But Jack didn't know that until he was grown. His mother used the elusive father to try to keep Jack in line as a boy.

You wouldn't act out like that if your father was around.

Rather than toe the line, Jack deliberately misbehaved, hoping his father would come back and give him the chance to be good.

Once he finally realized his father wasn't coming back, the bad-boy behavior was ingrained, and he simply played the part of bad boy because that's exactly what everyone expected of him.

The sun dropped below the horizon and the room darkened completely. He continued to soothe her, and Maddie buried her face in his shoulder. He wanted to kiss away her hurt, but refrained. Each time her body shook with sobs, he tried to calm her with words and a gentle touch.

Finally her body went limp and her breathing slowed, as she slid into a deep sleep. Jack inched to the edge of the sofa and with Maddie still in his arms, rose and carried her to her bed. He pulled the sheet over her, wishing he could lie beside her and keep her in his embrace.

Instead, he settled into a recliner in the corner, sleeping when Maddie slept and lying miserably awake each time she awoke in tears.

Take care of her, Jack. Promise me.

"Dammit, I'm trying. I'm trying," he whispered just before he drifted off to sleep again.

* * *

If Sunday had been hell, Monday was hell in triplicate.

Maddie pulled a bottle of eye drops from her purse and prayed they would work the miracle their manufacturer promised. Her still-puffy eyes and sore throat were visual reminders of the disappointment she had experienced when the cramping began and she saw the drops of blood. She wanted to be pregnant, and when her period had been a day late, she'd allowed herself to hope. She had imagined the upstairs bedroom with a delicate pink floral décor for a girl or a soft blue and white color scheme to suit a little boy.

She'd planned a Sunday afternoon excursion to one of the baby superstores nearby—just to look, just to see what might fit the vision she had for her baby's nursery.

As she'd dressed, the first mild twinge—hardly a pain at all—forced her to pause. When stronger cramps gripped her middle as she stood in the kitchen searching for a paper and pen to write a note for Jack, she abandoned her purse and keys, investigated the situation in her bathroom and then curled up on the sofa to wait for the pain tablets to take effect.

No pills could take away the pain in her heart or the deep, wrenching hurt in her soul. This loss brought back reminders of Alex's death and compounded the ache. When Jack had found her in the dark, he'd cradled her in his arms so gently and reassured her.

His tenderness surprised her, but it wasn't unwelcome. His comforting touch and talk had lulled her to sleep, and for a while she believed that everything *would* be okay as Jack had repeated while he held her.

But would it? Their attempt at baby-making had failed, and now all she had was a sham marriage.

She tilted her head back and squeezed the liquid into her irritated eyes, dabbing at the runaway excess with a tissue. She reached for the cup of tea from the shop around the corner, hoping the sweet, hot liquid would ease the rawness at the back of her throat.

What she really needed was about twelve straight hours of sleep—deep, uninterrupted rest to allow her body to recuperate. But since that wasn't going to happen anytime soon, she took another sip of tea and willed the caffeine to kick in.

A knock sounded just as Tess flung open the door and marched in.

"Don't you ever wait to be invited in?" Maddie asked in irritation. "What if I was in here with a client? Or a man?"

"Jami-with-an-i told me you looked like hell when you came in this morning but I wanted to see for myself to make sure," Tess said, referring to the firm's newly hired, fresh-out-of-college receptionist. "She thinks anyone over thirty is old, so I thought her version of looking like hell might just mean you had forgotten to wear eyeliner. But damned if she isn't right, Maddie. You look like the depths of hell."

"Nice to see you, too," Maddie croaked before taking another swallow.

Tess pulled a chair close to the desk and sat. "What's bothering you more? The fact the test said *Not Pregnant* or the kiss Jack planted on you at the Fire and Ice Friday night?"

"How—"

Tess folded her arms across her chest and leaned back. "The first one's simple—a matter of math. And the second? Let's just say I had an eyewitness report, and I got hot and bothered just hearing about it. Did Jack really grope you and try to suck your tonsils out in the middle of the ballroom?"

Maddie remained silent as the words sank in.

"Well, the silence tells me a lot."

Maddie massaged her temples as she formulated her reply. "The test wasn't negative, but before you jump to even more conclusions, I didn't have to use the test. I started yesterday afternoon. That's pretty much a de facto pregnancy test right there."

"And the other?" Tess raised a perfectly shaped eyebrow.

"He did not grope me. Whoever told you that obviously had too much to drink." Maddie rose and walked to the window; the remnants of morning rush hour traffic raced by under a sky as cloudy as her mood.

"What about the kiss?"

Maddie spun around to face her. "Why don't you just tell me what you heard and I'll either confirm or deny it, counselor."

"Testy, aren't we?"

"Lack of sleep will do it to you. You'd lose sleep too if…"

"If I had a handsome husband like Jack under my roof? You bet I would. Sex is so much more fun than sleep."

"It doesn't matter because he won't be living under my roof much longer."

"Did that bastard threaten to walk out because you didn't get pregnant?" Tess's temper flared.

"Testy, aren't we?" Maddie mimicked Tess's earlier words. "What happened to the Jack Worth Fan Club?"

"What did he do, Maddie?"

"He didn't do anything."

Liar.

He'd stayed in her bedroom with her all night, making sure she wasn't alone. She had wanted so desperately for him to lie down beside her and hold her tightly, and when he didn't take the initiative on his own, she had come very close to asking. She didn't want him to get the wrong idea, however. She didn't want things to get serious between them, couldn't let things get serious between them, because she would never put her heart on the line again. She had merely wanted the comfort of another human being.

Liar, liar.

Maddie had wanted Jack, not just any warm body. But Tess couldn't know that. Not after all the repeated declarations about their marriage being for convenience only.

The kiss was another matter. If Tess had heard about it, even though her details were a bit off, then it must have been as passionate as she remembered. It must have been as red hot as her face must have been when they'd been called out for their very public display of affection.

"Your silence is speaking again," Tess stated once more.

What the hell? Tess had to know eventually if she was going to draw up the paperwork.

"I'm going to give Jack a divorce. I'm going to let him off the hook." Maddie returned to her desk and sank into the large, executive style chair. "We tried and I didn't get pregnant, so I'm going to give him an out and let him go back to his bachelor ways."

"And what about your baby dreams?"

Sometimes dreams had to take a backseat to reality. And the reality was, she was afraid she could become too attracted to Jack Worth if she had to continue having sex with him. So attracted she might not want to ever walk away from him. It was far better to bail now while it was only about biology and not about emotions.

"I'll go back to my original idea and use the fertility clinic's sperm bank. I had a donor picked out and had started the whole process before Jack and I...you know."

"And what about Judge Ward?" Tess countered.

"I guess I'll deal with him if and when he becomes a problem. If I have to, I'll move somewhere else."

"And give up everything you have here?"

"What I have here won't matter if I can't do the work I love. So, will you draw up the paperwork for me? I don't want Jack to lose anything. You did a great job on the prenup so he should be okay. And I'll even sweeten the pot a little if I need to."

Tess sent her an appraising look. "Why don't you wait a week or two until the disappointment has worn off and maybe you'll change your mind. You haven't been married that long and you only tried once to get pregnant. You could try again. I hate to see you rush into a divorce when things get a little rough. I can recommend someone for you to talk to if you'd like."

Maddie slapped her palms on the desk and leaned forward. "I'm not one of your clients, Tess. You don't have to swoop in and save the day for me. I know what I'm doing. Jack knew what the deal was when he said 'I do' and he'll probably be glad to get away from the crazy hormonal woman anyway."

"All right. I'll add it to my schedule." Tess rose and walked resolutely to the door. She reached for the handle then paused to look back at Maddie.

"Then I guess what I heard about the kiss wasn't true after all. I heard that Jack looked like a man who had willingly given his heart to the woman in his arms and that the woman in his arms looked totally head over heels in love with her husband."

"No," Maddie said, steeling herself against the onslaught of emotion. "Not true at all."

Tess let herself out, closing the door with a quiet click, and Maddie surrendered to the tears that gathered behind her lids.

Not true at all.

And perhaps if she continued to repeat the lie she'd start to believe it herself.

* * *

Mondays had to be some higher power's idea of the ultimate punishment, and Jack had ticked off that higher power beyond all hope of reprieve. His jaw cracked as he yawned for the umpteenth time since he'd dragged his aching body from the chair in Maddie's bedroom at dawn. He'd hoped a hot shower and equally hot coffee would help, and they did just long enough to let him drive to work.

He had managed pretty well until lunch when he'd filled his stomach with a turkey club sandwich. Once his body had begun to digest the food, it decided sleep was in order and Jack had leaned back in his chair to close his eyes for just a minute. Then Millie had shaken him gently by the shoulder and snapped him out of his nap.

"Here's a fresh cup of coffee, boss," she said, setting his favorite mug on the desk in front of him. "I made it a little stronger than usual."

Jack lifted the mug to his lips, inhaled the aroma and drank. "Oh God, that's good." He set the cup back down, wiped at his eyes and blinked away the traces of sleep. "How long was I out?"

"Best I can tell, about an hour. If you and the missus are going to stay up until the wee hours of the night you should probably get that futon you've been talking about for the empty office. It would be a lot easier on your neck than sleeping at your desk."

"I wish," Jack muttered before another massive yawn split his face.

"You mean you weren't up all night making babies?" Millie asked, grinning like the proverbial Cheshire cat.

"No, I was up all night listening to her cry."

"What on earth did you do to that woman, Jack Worth?" She glowered at him and made him feel like a teenager caught sneaking in after curfew. "If you hurt her—so much as laid a finger on her—"

"Calm down," he ordered. "I hurt her, but not like you think."

"Start talking." She'd moved to the side of his desk and hovered over him.

"I didn't get her pregnant. She found out yesterday and well, it was a pretty long night."

"I hate to break up your pity party, but unless you know you have a problem in that department, it isn't necessarily your fault she didn't get pregnant. Not every couple gets pregnant the first time they try. You probably just didn't hit the right nights this time."

"Damn, I can't believe I'm talking about sex with you." Heat crept up his neck and his face burned. "You're old enough to be my—"

"Watch it," she warned.

"My mother's young friend," he said, placating no one because they both knew she was older than Connie.

"Trust me, honey, there's nothing you can tell me I haven't heard before. I've been around the block a time or two, and I can assure you Clayton and I did not have two sons by Immaculate Conception. Didn't they teach you anything in sex education class?"

"That might have been the day I cut class," he said, chuckling. "I did a lot of independent study projects that semester."

Millie whacked him across the shoulder with the back of her hand before pacing to the corner of his office and settling into a chair. "For once in your life, be serious, Jack."

He'd been serious the morning he and Maddie had made love. He'd been as serious as he knew how in trying to make sure he was convincing as a husband. And Lord knows, he'd been serious last night when he'd held Maddie and tried to comfort her.

"Tell me everything you did," she directed. "And we'll try to figure out what went wrong."

"No," he stated point blank. "I am not giving you a blow-by-blow description of my sex life."

Millie released an exaggerated sigh. "I don't mean that. Tell me how you decided which nights to have sex."

"Night. Which night to have sex."

A look of disbelief crossed Millie's face. "Are you telling me…"

He nodded soberly. "I should have known the old-fashioned way wouldn't work as well as the modern technology at a fertility clinic. All I did was make things awkward for Maddie and act like some rutting animal."

"I'll reserve comment on the rutting animal part, but you're wrong about the old-fashioned way. It's better than the fertility clinic."

"And you're an expert on this because…" His question faded away and he waited for her answer.

"I watch a lot of cable television."

Ah, hell. An armchair physician, and she was going to advise him on how to get a woman pregnant.

"Don't look at me like that. Look it up on the Internet. You'll see. And picking one night because you think that's when she's most fertile isn't very effective either. Have you ever been target shooting? It's kind of like that."

Jack nodded, wondering where the analogy was headed.

"If you only fire one bullet, you'd better have damn good aim if you expect to hit the target. But if you fire a whole box of bullets, you stand a much better chance of getting a bull's-eye."

Jack blinked, then picked up a pen and fidgeted with it.

"Don't you always say you need a back-up plan for any construction project in case plan A doesn't work?"

"Yes," he agreed, waiting for her to continue with her lecture on fertility and conception.

"So here's Plan B."

* * *

By the time Jack arrived home he knew more about fertility than he had ever wanted to know, but also knew exactly where they'd gone wrong. He'd also practiced saying the word orgasm until he could do it without being embarrassed.

Their one-bullet approach had left way too much room for error. Plan B would fire a salvo of bullets at her egg—not just one night, but every night for ten days.

The plan made perfect sense to him, but he had to be persuasive when he explained it to Maddie. Persuasive enough to convince her he wasn't just a horn-dog out to satisfy his libido, but that he honestly had her best interest at heart.

And that was the one little part he was most concerned about— *his* heart. Because it was going to be hell to make love to Maddie every day for a week and a half and not feel something more than pure physical release. He'd already felt his heart slip over the past month and it scared the shit out of him. He was just supposed to look out for her, and that had morphed into a pregnancy negotiation. Now he would be putting lots more on the line—provided she agreed.

She had beaten him home and was seated at the kitchen table when he walked in. He really wanted to have a stiff drink and maybe a cold shower before he broached the subject with her, but the longer he waited, the more difficult the conversation would become.

"We need to talk, Jack," she said before he even made it to the table.

Maybe she'd come to the same conclusion as he had, or heaven forbid, maybe Millie had called her and talked about Plan B even though she had promised not to.

"Okay," he said, pulling out a chair and straddling it.

"I spoke to Tess today about starting divorce proceedings. We can just tell everyone we rushed into marriage and it didn't work out."

His forehead wrinkled in surprise and he felt the bottom begin to drop out of his world.

"Divorce?" he asked incredulously. "After we've been telling them for the past two weeks that we knew we were madly in love and didn't want to wait any longer to tie the knot?"

Maddie frowned at him. "This whole situation is complicated enough as it is. There's no need to confuse matters more. We gave the pregnancy thing our best shot, Jack, and it just didn't work out. I don't want you to feel obligated any further. You did your part and I can't ask any more of you."

"Wait, wait, wait, wait, wait. You're making this sound like I signed up for a one-time-only opportunity."

Maddie stared at him in surprise. "Didn't you?"

"Sweetheart, I'm in this for the long haul. I'm here until you get pregnant." He pulled a folded sheet of paper from his back pocket and smoothed it out on the table. "I spent the afternoon trying to figure out where we went wrong and this is what I found."

He explained Plan B to her. "And that's my best and final offer," he said sincerely.

A weak smile turned up the corners of her mouth, and despite the renewed tears, she seemed to be relieved.

As much as anyone might think he was in this arrangement just to have sex with a beautiful woman without any commitments, Jack knew deep inside that it was more than that. It wasn't about the sex anymore.

It was a hell of a lot more.

It was about his soul.

Nine

Was Jack trying to con her—trying his hardest to weasel his way into her bed on a nightly basis? Or was he sincere about helping her? Trying to figure out the answer had her tossing and turning and afraid of losing another night's sleep, even though the numbers on her alarm clock showed it was only ten o'clock.

She had been ready to walk away. She had convinced herself she needed to regain her privacy. She wanted to be able to close all the blinds and walk around the house in her nightgown. Be in her own home and not constantly feel Jack's gaze on her.

Liar.

If she could object to the voice in her head, she would. She'd get a protective order to keep it away where it couldn't remind her that despite her best efforts she was becoming emotionally involved with Jack.

Their one-night arrangement had wreaked enough havoc with her emotions, but this new plan of his? Ten nights of sex?

Not that any sane woman would complain about being the object of such a good lover's attentions. Many women would consider Maddie's situation to be quite enviable, and those same women would call her ten kinds of a fool for wanting out of it.

She had managed to paint herself a picture of Jack as the bad guy—the man who made her doubt her own decisions, used coercion and bribery, and then two weeks later embarrassed her in front of Atlanta society at the Fire and Ice ball. And when she'd been ready to cut him loose, he'd delivered an impassioned speech about promises and commitment and being there for the long haul.

Damn him to hell.

She punched her pillow again and peeked at the clock one more time. Ten minutes after ten.

But her own research had turned up the same information he had presented to her, frequent intercourse made more sense than charting and testing and turning the whole event into one giant science project.

No, she was going to have to erase that picture of the bad guy and replace it, because what could possibly be so bad about nightly sex with Jack? Handsome, virile, maddeningly sexy and attractive

Jack. Everything. That's what. But if she wanted a baby, she would have to agree to the new plan. She couldn't dump any of the blame on Jack for the emotional rollercoaster she was riding. This was all on her.

Maddie threw back the sheet and sat on the side of the bed. She jammed her feet into her slippers and groped at the bottom of the bed for her robe.

She made her way through the family room and kitchen, then tiptoed down the basement stairs and knocked at the door of Jack's domain. Given her pulse rate and the churning in her stomach, there might as well have been a sign over the door warning her to abandon all hope if she entered. That or a notice that a wild animal lived behind the door. From what she'd experienced with Jack so far, either caveat could be true.

He flung open the door and waved her in. "Have you come to your senses and decided to agree with me?"

He wore a pair of cut-off sweatpants but no shirt. A towel hung around his neck and a fine sheen of perspiration covered his body. Looking past him, she saw the display blinking on the elliptical trainer he'd brought with him.

She avoided answering by walking to the middle of the room and turning slowly to inspect it. She'd only been in the basement one other time since the day she'd helped him move in. She also avoided looking at him because the sweatpants rode low on his hips and revealed the chiseled body she remembered running her hands over.

A line of dark hair started at his navel and drew her gaze to the point where it disappeared beneath his cut-offs. It pointed the way to pleasure and made her want to sing "Happy Trails."

"It's surprisingly neat," she said. "I sort of expected beer can pyramids and old pizza boxes. Maybe tighty-whities on the back of the sofa."

"I don't wear briefs."

She was tempted to ask what he did wear, but refrained. "It's nice down here."

"First of all, I'm a guest in your house, so I feel a need to keep it clean. Second, I'm insulted by your gross generalization based on my gender." He ticked off his points on the fingers of his left hand. "Did you come here for some reason other than to insult me?"

"You're not making this easy," she began.

A muscle twitched in his jaw. "Most of the best things in life never are," he said, clearly annoyed. He pulled the towel from around his neck, wiped his face and chest and then tossed it on the back of a dining chair. "There. Feel better?"

Hell was too good for him. Thoughts of honey and a mound of fire ants raced through her mind.

"I know you didn't come down here for dorm inspection, so…"

"I've thought about your proposition and I came to…" Maddie's throat tightened at the enormity of what she was about to say. She took a deep breath and blew it out. "I've decided to tell Tess to hold off on that thing I talked to her about."

"A divorce," he stated matter-of-factly.

"Yes, a divorce. She suggested I wait a few weeks and let my emotions calm down, so when I tell her I've changed my mind, she'll just think I'm taking her advice."

"And my other suggestion?"

"I've given it a lot of thought and done my own research." She paced back and forth in front of the French doors leading to the patio. "Intellectually, I know your way is the right thing to do. Your bullet theory does have some basis in fact. But on the other hand…"

Did she really want to admit to Jack that she was both afraid and thrilled about the idea of having him in her bed every night? Making love with Jack had shaken her up even as it had awakened her long-dormant libido.

"It's not *my* way. This is a generally recognized fertility method. Look at it like this, Maddie," he began, stepping closer, which allowed her to see just how developed his biceps really were. "Daily sex gives you the optimum chance at getting pregnant. And if you like, I can show you some information about other things to increase your chances even more."

"Other things?" She crossed her arms defensively across her chest.

"Different positions."

Her breathing quickened and an unwelcome flush crept up her neck and face.

"And remember that *pleasure* I insisted you have?"

She nodded, wondering which dark alley the conversation would wander down now.

"It appears I was a fertility genius and didn't know it." He waggled his eyebrows and grinned boldly. "Orgasm contractions help carry sperm further into a woman's body, so it's kinda like firing bullets with an assault rifle rather than a Derringer."

Embarrassed, Maddie wished someone would just shoot her now, and it didn't matter to her what kind of gun they used.

"This method just lets the law of averages prevail," he continued, moving a little closer. "You're an attorney, Maddie. Don't you believe in the law?"

"Yes," she said, taking a step backwards and bumping into one of the recliners.

"Yes, you believe? Or yes to having sex every night?"

She shoved her hair back from her face and squared her shoulders. "Both. So I guess you'll start coming upstairs the weekend after next?"

Jack laughed aloud and Maddie realized what she'd said.

Damn him to the hottest part of hell. She couldn't even make a simple statement without him attaching some dirty connotation to it.

"That's something else I wanted to talk to you about. Another proposition." His expression sobered.

"Do tell." Instead of the rational conversation she'd expected, now she was engaged in an exchange filled with bawdy innuendo and double entendres, and she already knew she was way out of her league. "Do you want to add whips and chains to the mix now? Maybe a little black leather?"

"No, nothing as exotic as that, though if you're open to kinky stuff, I'll put them on the short list of sexual preferences." She would have panicked had she not seen the wink that accompanied his remark.

"What I'd like to discuss is location."

"Location," she repeated in a worried tone. "Is this in any way related to different positions?"

"Play your cards right and it could be."

Maddie sidestepped and turned toward the stairs. "I'm going back to bed now. I think I might be getting a headache. We'll finish this discussion when you can be serious."

And when you put on a shirt so I'm not distracted by your body.

Jack reached for her arm but grabbed a handful of her robe instead. "Aww, you're hurting my feelings."

She spun to face him. "Yeah, right. I should just forget this—"

"I'm sorry. Really. Please don't leave until we've settled this. I promise I'll be serious, because this is a very serious matter."

She tugged her robe from his grasp and pulled it tighter around her. "Yeah, sure. That's what you always say."

"I mean it this time. I swear. But I'd be a lot more comfortable if I was clean," he said. "Would you mind waiting while I take a shower? I won't be long. You can watch TV or look at a magazine or—"

"How about a cup of hot chocolate? If you don't have any, I can get some from my kitchen."

"Sounds great. If you don't mind the instant kind, I have some packets in the cabinet over the stove."

Maddie listened to the sound of running water and imagined Jack wet and naked while she waited for the kettle to boil. When Jack stepped into the small kitchen, dressed in athletic shorts and a T-shirt and smelling like some sort of sporty soap, she was stirring two steaming mugs.

"After you," he said, taking one mug and following her to the sofa. He sat on one end and propped his bare feet on the coffee table, crossing them at the ankle.

Maddie sat on the opposite end, her legs tucked underneath her, sipping cocoa and sneaking glances at him. His wet hair was combed back from his face and a drop of water crawled down his neck toward the ribbed crew neck of his shirt. She fought the urge to lean over and wipe it away.

"As I was saying when I so rudely veered off in the wrong direction, I'd like to ask you if we could have sex somewhere besides your bedroom."

"Why? What's wrong with my bedroom?"

Jack rubbed his hand across his jaw, shadowed by a day's growth of beard. "I don't know any way to say this but to be perfectly honest. I'm just not real comfortable having sex with you in the same bed where you slept with your former husband."

"Oh." Until now, she had no idea being in the bed she had shared with Alex would bother Jack. She had only considered her own feelings. Of course he would feel awkward and this was an entirely rational and acceptable argument. "Then where?"

He nodded toward the bedroom and his grin flashed briefly before he doused it.

Jack's bedroom? His bed? She opened her mouth to speak but he spoke before she could.

"It's too far to commute to the cabin, and renting a motel room every night would get expensive unless we wanted to go to a place that rents by the hour."

She inhaled raggedly and dribbled her drink down her chin.

"I'm joking, Maddie," he said, moving over to swipe at the chocolaty smudge with his thumb. "But look at it from my perspective. Would you want to know that other women had been in the bed where you were making love to your husband?"

The thought had crossed her mind. How many women had Jack bedded in that king-size pleasure palace in the next room?

He nodded toward the bedroom. "You might find it hard to believe, but there's never been a woman in that bed," he said, as if reading her mind.

She thought back to the day Jack had moved in. "Well, of course not. You bought it when you moved in here."

Jack drained his mug and leaned to place it on the coffee table. "I'm going to let you in on a little secret, Maddie. Not only has there never been a woman in that bed, until you and I had sex at the cabin, I've been celibate since before Alex died."

The shock of this bombshell hit her full force and left her too stunned to react. Here was one more instance where she had misjudged Jack. That list was growing longer daily.

He leaned back, his hands locked together behind his head. "Running Prescott-Worth was a full-time job for two men, and when he got too sick to work, I practically ate and slept at the office. Between that and donat—" He quieted suddenly.

"I know about that. Millie told me you donated platelets for him as often as you could."

An irritated expression crossed his face.

"Don't be mad at her. She was worried I'd be mad because you missed a morning of work every ten days or so."

Maddie reached for his hand. "I appreciate everything you did to keep the company going," she said softly. "I should have said something before now."

He shrugged one shoulder. "It's okay. You've had a lot on your plate."

She studied Jack's profile; the square jaw, the stubborn set of his chin, the slight imperfection of his nose that hinted at a fist-fight or two. His skin was tanned to a rich bronze from hours outside on job sites, and the sun had added gold streaks to his chestnut-brown hair. No wonder Tess thought he was a hottie.

He was.

Jack Worth was an in-the-flesh, certified hunk and he was hers for the asking. And that brought her right back to being both scared and excited about having him in her bed.

Correction. Being in *his* bed.

She had agreed to his plan—all parts of it—and now she needed to get back upstairs to *her* bed. Tomorrow she would tell Tess to cancel the divorce paperwork—at least for now. Eventually she and Jack would go their separate ways, but for now they would remain man and wife, and in five days they would start trying to make a baby again.

"I guess I had better get back to sleep. I'm beat from not sleeping well last night." She rose from the sofa.

His hand snaked out and took her by the wrist. "Stay with me, Maddie."

"I couldn't," she said softly. "I can't. I mean, it's not time yet."

"I know. It won't be about sex. We'll just be sharing the bed—sort of a practice run for the real thing without really practicing." He pulled her closer and placed his mouth close to her ear. "It'll give you a chance to get used to my snoring."

She smacked his shoulder then laughed nervously before burying her face against his chest until she could regain her composure. She had given in willingly, and, in addition to his snoring, she had a feeling she'd get used to his electrifying touch and the way it made her heart hammer.

* * *

Jack tugged her toward the lighted bedroom and interpreted her lack of resistance to mean she had agreed to stay. He wasn't sure what had made him ask her, especially when he had already spooked her with his other requests. He just knew he wanted her beside him tonight. He wanted to hear her breathing from the other side of the bed, to know he wasn't alone. To know he hadn't scared her off completely with his demands.

"Do you prefer one side over the other?" he asked, pulling his shirt over his head. He started to drop it on the floor but instead he tossed it in the laundry basket in the corner.

"I usually sleep on the side closest to the bathroom," she answered, pointing to the right side of the large bed. "But the lamp's on that side so it must be where you sleep…" Her voice trailed off and he could see the uneasy expression that crossed her face.

"That's fine. Take that side," he said and yawned. "Let me go lock up and turn out the lights."

When he returned a few minutes later, Maddie's robe was draped across the bottom of the bed and she was tucked safely under the covers.

"Is the alarm already set or do I need…?" She stopped mid-sentence as Jack skimmed his shorts over his hips to the floor and crawled into bed. "Don't you normally put on pajamas? Didn't you sleep in lounge pants at the cabin?"

He chuckled as she edged closer to the far side of the mattress. "Usually don't wear them." He settled beneath the covers on his side of the bed and punched the pillow several times. "It helps keep my laundry at a manageable level."

"I'll bet you don't wear underwear either."

"How'd you guess?" He winked at her before turning on his side, facing away from her. "Turn out the light, would you?"

* * *

Maddie flushed the toilet and washed her hands, hurrying back to crawl into the bed.

"Are you okay?" Jack's voice was thick with sleep.

"Yeah. Just a bathroom call. I'm sorry I woke you." She pulled the sheet to her chin and shivered in the nighttime chill.

"Are you cold?" he asked, turning toward her.

"A little, but I'll warm up." Admitting she was cold was an invitation for her naked bed mate to offer to warm her up, and that was not what she wanted.

Liar, her conscience nagged again. Maybe if he slid to her side of the bed just a little and trapped her cold toes between his warm feet she'd be able to go back to sleep.

As if he could read her mind, he maneuvered to her side of the bed. Way over on her side. "Come here, sweetheart. Move in close to me."

But he's naked, her conscience badgered once more before giving in. She snuggled close, soaking in the warmth of his body. "Oh my gosh, you're so hot."

When Jack began to shake with laughter, her body flushed from sheer mortification.

"I mean…your body. It's hot. In the bed. Temperature-wise that is. Oh God, can I possibly dig myself any deeper into a hole?"

Jack let the laughter burst to the surface. "I know what you mean," he said when he finally caught his breath.

Maddie wasn't sure if that made her feel better or not. Their arrangement was purely business. It wouldn't do for her to give him the wrong idea.

Nonetheless, she relaxed into the warmth of his arms and began drifting back to sleep. He pressed a light kiss to her temple and adjusted his arm under her.

"For what it's worth," he murmured, "I think you're pretty hot, too."

She struggled for the right words, but abandoned the effort in favor of sleep.

"Goodnight, Maddie. Sleep tight."

She certainly would.

* * *

The last week had been a giant lesson in self-control for Jack. Every night he had prepared dinner for Maddie. According to his research, she could aid conception by avoiding processed foods and eating a diet rich in fresh fruits and vegetables, dairy products and lean protein.

Right now he'd kill for a tub of fried chicken with mashed potatoes and gravy and a couple of beers, but instead he'd grilled fish and prepared a green salad. He set their places in the dining room rather than in the kitchen, and he had added some candles he'd found in a drawer. Alcohol was forbidden so he'd filled their wine glasses with sparkling grape juice.

"Come and get it," he called from the dining room. She was barefoot so he didn't realize she was behind him until he heard the gasp of surprise when she saw the candles and the vase of fresh flowers he'd picked up at the grocery store.

Tonight was the launch of Plan B and Jack wanted to put Maddie at ease. He'd worried his fancy dinner might come across as the actions of a man more concerned with sex than conception. Only time would tell.

"This is beautiful," she said as he pulled out a chair for her. "And I love salmon."

It was good for her, too, but he'd keep that bit of information to himself. Tonight he wanted a relaxed atmosphere because stress hindered conception, and wasn't conceiving the whole point of all this?

He sat across from her—too far away in his estimation. Now he regretted the decision to go for the more formal setting instead of the cozier surroundings in the kitchen. Damn, but this whole sex thing was making him question his own judgment. Seduction had never been a problem for him before, and wasn't that what he needed to do tonight? Seduce Maddie?

Sure, she'd agreed to his sex marathon plan and to the change of venue he suggested. He'd spent more time upstairs with her than before, and on the previous weekend she had joined him downstairs in front of the big screen TV to watch a movie.

Meals and movies, however, were a far cry from rolling around naked in bed together. The night she'd spent with him repeated often in his dreams, and when he'd wake up hard and wanting her, Jack would stumble to the shower and let cold water sluice over his body. Then he would return to the bed that triggered the whole incident and more likely than not, end up aroused again.

He had been like a horny teenager who lusted after the prom queen and had to keep it a big secret. Only tonight he could let the cat out of the bag—or more accurately, he could give his raging libido room to rage just a little.

"Jack?" Her voice pulled him from his thoughts. "Is something wrong?"

He shook his head, smiled and filled his fork with another bite of food. Unfortunately, his mind was screaming otherwise. That horny teenager wanted to lay the prom queen across the vacant end of the dining room table and well…lay her right there. He willed his body to relax and his brain to stop sending signals to the southern hemisphere.

"I'll clean up," she offered when they'd both had their fill. "You cooked after all."

"It's good practice. Once we get you pregnant and the baby is born, you'll be too busy to cook but you still need to eat properly."

Her cheeks stained with color. Evidently she had a major case of nerves as well.

She stacked their plates and silverware and carried them to the sink. With a puff of breath, Jack extinguished the candles and followed with the rest, stepping behind her to set the glasses on the counter. She turned abruptly and collided with him. Their shared awareness of each other was palpable and he lost the tenuous grip he had on his control.

He framed her face with his hands and lowered his lips to hers. He demanded entrance to her mouth and swept his tongue inside. Drinking in her sweetness, he inched closer, surrendering to his desire, giving in to the anticipation that had eaten at him since their last night together.

Maddie released a sigh of pleasure and wrapped her arms around his neck. Her hip brushed against his fly and stripped him of all control.

He deepened the kiss and when she sighed again he tunneled under her top, bracketing her torso with his hands and letting his thumbs rest just below her breasts.

She buried her face against his chest then stood on tiptoe and seared a path along his jaw with her kisses. His erection slammed against his fly and he feared his jeans might do serious damage if he didn't get them off soon.

"Can we take this downstairs now?" His gruff whisper broke the silence.

"I thought you'd never ask," she said, kissing down his neck.

Sweeping her into his arms, he carefully made his way downstairs and into his bedroom. He set her down beside the bed and his gaze raked seductively from head to toe. His body ached for her touch, and he ached to be inside her, but he would let her take the lead.

She grasped the hem of her shirt and pulled it up and over her head. Jack instinctively reached to slide his hand across her silken skin. He eased his fingers to the lacy edge of her bra where her breast mounded above the fabric. He traced the scalloped edge slowly, filled with raw lust and longing, raking his fingers boldly down her body.

"So beautiful. So sexy." His voice barely audible, he rubbed his thumbs across the silk cups of her bra and her nipples responded to his touch. When he twisted the front closure open and her breasts spilled into his hands, he cupped them tenderly.

He lifted his gaze and studied her face, focusing on her angular features, her full lips and the long, dark lashes resting against her cheeks.

"Look at me, Maddie," he urged. When she opened her eyes, he saw his own longing reflected in them. He had waited for her and the prolonged anticipation had frustrated him. Relieved, now he knew the wait was over.

"I want you, Maddie. I want to be on top of you, inside of you. Now." The time for coy flirtation had passed.

He hooked his thumbs in the waistband of her lounge pants and shoved the fabric down until it puddled at her feet. She stepped out of the pants and he kicked them aside.

"You didn't wear underwear."

"I thought I'd follow your lead." She smiled wickedly, her excitement reflected in her eyes.

He stepped back and undid the button on his jeans, then slid the zipper down carefully. He toed off his shoes and yanked his socks off. The jeans followed quickly. Carefully he eased her backward until her legs bumped the mattress. Easing her onto the bed, he crawled in beside her, worshiping her body with every sense—the silken feel of her skin, the aroma of her floral perfume, the sight of her dark hair against the white sheets, the sound of her moans as he began his assault on her body.

Threading his fingers through hers, he pinned her to the bed and scorched a path of kisses down her body. He kissed each eyelid, the tip of her nose and sipped from her lips, swollen from the kisses in the kitchen.

He nibbled her neck and then returned to her breasts, flush with arousal and need. He shifted to begin the next phase of his assault and lost contact with her body.

* * *

Maddie's eyes flew open as he moved away from her. "Don't leave. Not now."

"I'm not going anywhere, sweetheart. I promise."

He wrapped one arm around her waist and pulled her closer and moved in for another kiss that was slow and thoughtful. He nibbled, then nipped playfully and Maddie returned his actions in kind. Then his mouth descended more firmly and the kiss morphed from yielding to firm, from playful to demanding, from unhurried to urgent.

His calloused hand cradled her face reverently and she saw desire in his eyes that had never been there before. Desire that mirrored her own. This man she'd viewed as merely a means to an end had become more—much more.

"Touch me," she commanded, asking him for the pleasure she had resisted before.

"Here?" he asked, fondling her breast lovingly, teasing the nipple until it firmed beneath his touch. "Or here?" The hand, which wielded a hammer so forcefully, circled her navel. "Or here?" He lowered his head and kissed the nipple he'd worried to a peak. She moaned her approval, and he drew the nipple into his mouth, treating her to sweet torture.

"Or maybe here?" he asked again, moving his hand between her thighs to her moist curls. He moved his fingers against the part of her body that wept for him and elicited another moan. When she arched her back and pressed her body against his hand, he gently slid a finger inside. He worked the finger in and out, using his thumb to stimulate her until she flew apart under his ministrations.

"That's one for you," he whispered, and his hot breath blew against her ear, arousing her further.

"And now it's your turn." She pushed to a sitting position. Maddie wanted to make sure Jack enjoyed the sex, too, wanted to make sure it wasn't purely duty on his part, though she doubted men could separate the two. Using both hands, she pushed him onto his back and straddled his hips.

"Nice turn," he commented, grinning broadly.

"You ain't seen nothing yet, babe." She leaned forward and kissed his forehead, her breasts brushing against his chest.

"And you're killing me, babe." He responded by grasping her hips and pulling her against his erection.

"Remember?" She punctuated her words with more kisses to his lips, his neck, his flat nipples. "It's all about guns?" She licked a path down his abdomen, traced the fine line of hair below his navel and heard him suck in a breath as she neared his groin.

"Just make sure you don't pull the trigger too soon."

She lapped at him, tasting him, and then took him in her mouth until he protested and pushed her away.

"Was I getting trigger happy?" She smiled seductively, delighted she had been able to excite him and also delighted he had stopped her.

"I'm just operating on a very short fuse here," he admitted, rubbing his hands up and down her back. "And we don't want to waste the swimmers, you know." He winked and Maddie felt her heart unlock and let him in.

She wrapped her hand around him, guided him to her wet core and lowered onto him. He filled her completely and she sighed, forgetting their coupling was for anything but sheer bliss.

Jack slid one hand from her hip to the point where they joined and massaged her again until she begged him to stop. He shifted, tilting their positions slightly, and raised his hips, thrusting deep and driving her to an intense climax.

She contracted around him, gripping him until he arched one last time and breathed her name on a satisfied sigh. She collapsed against him, feeling boneless from the exquisite pleasure, and wondering how she would ever be able to leave the comfort of his embrace.

* * *

"How did you meet Alex?" she asked as he cradled her in his arms. "All he would ever tell me is you were young and, well, stupid."

Jack chuckled. "That's pretty accurate. I'd even go so far as to say I was dumber than dirt. God, it's a miracle I lived to see my eighteenth birthday."

"Did you grow up in Atlanta?"

"Not Atlanta proper. My mom and I lived near the airport in a trailer park. She worked as a waitress—when she worked. If she could find a guy to move in and support us, she'd quit work until he moved out. And then she'd go back to the coffee shop and the cycle would repeat."

"What about your father?"

Jack remained silent for several minutes, unsure of just how much truth to share.

"I don't know," he said softly, shifting so he could see her face.

"You don't know where he is?"

He paused again even though the words didn't hurt as much now as they had when he'd first heard them fifteen years ago.

"I don't know *who* he is."

"Oh, Jack. I'm sorry. If I'd known—"

"It's okay. Actually, my father is a very significant part of how I met Alex."

Her forehead wrinkled in confusion. "I don't understand. If you didn't know who he was, how did that lead you to Alex?"

"All my life my mother repeated one line to me: *you wouldn't act out like that if your father was around.* She used this mystery man to try and keep me in line. But I'd just misbehave more, because in my mind I thought if I *was* deliberately bad, he'd come back home to give me the chance to be good. Needless to say, he never came back. I became known as the neighborhood bad boy. By the time I was in middle school, I'd started smoking and sneaking beer."

"But you don't smoke now."

"Hang on. That part's coming. When I was old enough I started working in fast food places, usually a different one every three to four months because my smart mouth would get me fired. But I managed to save enough to buy a car and keep the tank filled with gas. By eighteen, I was an expert bad boy because that's what everyone expected from me. I had hooked up with some guys who did carpentry work and odd jobs and I was making decent money working with them. I was tired of living at home and thought I was ready to move out and take on the world."

"I think most of us go through that phase."

"Yeah, but most people are smart enough to know their limits. Anyway, a week after graduation, and I use that term loosely because my grades just barely earned me a diploma, I found a place to live—a dump of an apartment on the east side of town, and I was packing my stuff to move. My mother came in tipsy, saw what I was doing and started a tirade about how every man she ever cared about had abandoned her and now I was doing the same thing."

Jack paused, remembering the confrontation clearly. "We argued and I opened my big mouth and said maybe if she hadn't been such a drunk and a nag my father wouldn't have moved out, too.

"That's when she dropped the bomb and told me she had no idea who my father was. Maybe it was Mr. Friday Night or maybe Mr. Saturday Afternoon. Or it could have been the Sunday morning guy or the Sunday nooner or even her landlord she screwed at three every Sunday afternoon while his wife went to visit her mother."

Maddie stilled in his arms and he glanced her way to see if he had either shocked her into silence or put her to sleep with his soap opera tale. Instead, he saw her eyes filled with tears. "I had no idea," she said in a broken whisper.

"It's not exactly the sort of thing you talk about at cocktail parties," he said wryly. "Anyway, I stormed out, got into a bar with a fake ID and I got rip-snorting drunk. I was mad at my mother, mad at the son of a bitch who let me go through life without a father and mad at the world in general. I wanted to hit somebody or something and one of Alex's projects got in my way. It was that apartment complex he helped construct before he got into residential construction."

"In College Park," she offered. "He showed it to me one time."

"That's the one. I had trashed one unit and had started on the second when Alex drove up. He tried to stop me and I damn near broke his arm fighting back. Then I puked all over his boots and really endeared myself to him." Jack remembered all too well the angry kid he'd been. "He hauled me to the foreman's trailer to call the cops and I passed out on the sofa. And when I woke up the next morning, I was in a bed in a house instead of in a jail cell."

"He took you home with him?" she asked in disbelief.

Jack nodded. "Apparently my boyish charm and good looks got to him and he decided not to press charges—at least not if I did everything he demanded."

"He blackmailed you?"

"He sure did. Where do you think I learned the fine art of extortion?" Another memory darted through his head, of Maddie and him in the cabin.

Maddie yawned and he glanced at the bedside clock. "I need to let you get some sleep."

"No, tell me the rest of the story," she begged, unsuccessful at stifling another yawn.

"Okay, here's the condensed version. I got the Alex Prescott version of community service for vandalism, public intoxication and underage drinking. Oh, and for puking on his new boots. If I worked off the damage—and it was a hell of a lot of damage—he said he wouldn't turn me in to the cops. By the time I'd sobered up and realized what I'd done, I was scared enough to take him up on his offer. The next year he helped me enroll at Georgia State and we eventually became partners. I still have no idea why he decided to give me a chance instead of turning my sorry ass over to the police. It would have been a lot easier and cheaper for him."

"He was a good judge of character."

"And I was a hell of a character back then."

"You're still a hell of a character."

"And you need to go to sleep," he told her when she yawned again.

* * *

Jack lay in the dark, trying to sleep, thoughts whirring through his brain. Thoughts of how soft her skin was and how she'd melted in his embrace. How tight she'd been when he pushed inside her and how she'd fought the pleasure then surrendered and enjoyed it. How she'd sighed deeply when she came apart in his arms.

How it had been so long since the last time he'd been with a woman before Maddie. How he'd enjoyed the hell out of being inside her, of having her on top of him, and now he was going straight to hell for falling in love when he was supposed to be protecting her and helping her.

She was in his bed where he'd wanted her all along. Was it selfish? Absolutely. Even a bit manipulative. But she'd been uninhibited and he knew for damn sure she'd have never been that way upstairs. Their arrangement might be "business," but Jack had never shied away from mixing in a little pleasure.

Before Maddie, sex had always been for the sake of recreation rather than for procreation, and he'd found the latter to be an almost spiritual experience. Oh yeah, that was him all right.

Saint Jack.

Ten

"Oh, hell, Tess, what have I gotten myself into?" Maddie picked the olives off a slice of greasy pizza and chewed off a big bite. So much for the nutritious breakfast she was supposed to eat. Jack would lecture her into next week if he knew what she was shoving in her mouth. But what Jack didn't know wouldn't hurt him.

What had begun as a work meeting had quickly deteriorated into something closer to a counseling session than a legal pow-wow.

"Would this have anything to do with the situation you let your ticking ovaries get you into?"

"My ovaries aren't ticking." Maddie dipped a piece of pizza crust into a cup of marinara sauce and popped it into her mouth.

Tess lifted one perfectly arched eyebrow and nailed her with a look of disbelief.

"Okay, so maybe they're chiming on the hour," Maddie conceded. "But that's not the problem."

"Do you think you got pregnant?" Tess asked.

Maddie paused, ready to tell Tess the subject was off limits but reconsidered. Tess was her best friend. Her ally. For heaven's sake, Tess was her accomplice in this whole affair. "I don't know."

"Do you feel pregnant?"

"I don't know," Maddie repeated. "How does pregnant feel?"

"You got me there. I just thought maybe you were puking every morning or something."

Maddie paused mid-bite. "It's ten in the morning, we're eating re-heated leftover pizza with everything including pineapple and anchovies and you're asking if I have morning sickness?"

"Maybe you're one of those women who don't get sick. Maybe you just have strange cravings like…"

Maddie considered the food in her hand and dropped the pizza slice back onto the napkin. Pineapple and anchovies. How much stranger could pizza get?

"Can we drop this subject, please?"

Tess shrugged and took another bite. "So what else have you gotten into that has you cussing like a sailor?"

Maddie sent her friend a disapproving look. "One *hell* isn't cussing like a sailor."

142

"Just to be safe, you need to start putting a dollar in some kind of container every time you say a bad word." Tess rose and moved to the bookcase against the wall. "This'll do," she said, holding out a coffee mug emblazoned with the firm's logo.

"Judge Ward apparently has no problems with my quickie marriage. He gave me a new case today. It's striking a little too close to home for comfort." Maddie reached for a folder in her inbox. "Oh, hell, Tess. You don't think he knows, do you?"

Tess set the mug on Maddie's desk with a thump. "That'll be a dollar. You'll thank me later when your kid starts talking and parrots every word you say." She folded herself back into the chair across from Maddie. "Only four people know the truth. I haven't told anyone and you haven't. I don't believe Jack would and Millie—"

"Millie would die to protect Jack. I'm just paranoid, I guess."

"Could you recuse yourself from the case?"

"On what grounds? That I can't be objective about a sperm donor coming back ten years later and wanting visitation with the son he helped create because Ward thinks I'm scared my sperm donor might do the same thing to me if I get pregnant?"

"Well, yeah." Tess wiped her fingers on a paper napkin. "Although, technically speaking, you don't have a sperm donor. You have a husband."

"And I wouldn't have one if my other husband hadn't made a deathbed request that my current husband felt obligated to fulfill by going over and above the call of duty." Maddie leaned back in her desk chair and stared at the ceiling. "What I wouldn't give to be able to roll back time a couple of years."

"Let's just say that was possible. What would you have done differently given the same set of circumstances with Alex's health?"

Maddie closed her eyes and considered Tess's question. Deep inside she knew the answer. There wasn't a thing she could or would have changed. She wouldn't have pushed to have a baby, wouldn't have worked less or asked Alex to give less than his all to his business.

"Nothing."

"I didn't think so," Tess replied.

"Of course there are plenty of things I could have done differently over the past year. For one, I could have been a little less dense. Figured out why Jack kept inviting me to dinner every month and put an end to it ages ago. I could have told Jack to take his sense of obligation and shove it. And I definitely should have said no to his sperm."

"And do you think he'd have walked away? He doesn't strike me as the kind of man who makes many promises, but I'll bet he keeps the ones he makes. Alex didn't want you to hole up in that big house and hide from the world. That's what Jack was trying to keep you from doing."

"I just keep wondering why Alex thought I needed to be taken care of. I mean, I have a great job—most of the time. I'm in good shape financially. I keep asking myself what was going through his mind when he asked Jack to hover over me. Was he even in his right mind? You know how much morphine they had him on at the end. Did he realize he was throwing Jack and me together?"

"Maddie, honey. You can second-guess things all you want, but nothing can change the fact that Alex is dead, and you're alive and married to that hunk of a man. Is there a problem with that?"

"Only one. I…" Maddie sighed deeply and fiddled with an errant piece of pepperoni.

"You're in love with him. I knew it!" Tess pumped her fist in the air.

"Is it that obvious?"

"Only to your best friend. But newlyweds are supposed to look like they're in love, so I wouldn't worry about that too much."

Maddie covered her face with both hands and despair washed over her. "But I'm not supposed to be in love with him. How on earth did I let this happen?"

"Do you think having sex with the man every night might have had something to do with it?" Tess unsuccessfully tried to stifle a laugh. "Have you considered that maybe you should forget that you're not supposed to fall in love and just go ahead and let it happen? Who knows? Maybe he'll fall, too."

"Oh, I don't think so. He's made it pretty clear he's a no-commitment kind of guy. He's a sperm donor and that's all." Maddie held up her left hand and the diamond ring sparkled in the light. "This was only to protect my job."

"Lots of sperm donors have changed their minds when they see their baby for the first time."

"And then there's Garrett Bates."

"Who's he?"

"The sperm donor for my newest client, ten-year-old Dylan Stewart. Bates has appeared out of nowhere and asked for visitation privileges with Dylan. Judge Ward appointed me as the GAL."

"Didn't his parents have an anonymity clause?"

Maddie shook her head. "It gets even better. The father and Bates were a couple years apart in med school. It was a do-it-yourself insemination with a verbal agreement. The couple needed sperm and didn't have much money to pay for it, and the donor was willing to take what the parents offered. They all went their separate ways and now Bates has decided he wants to get to know his flesh and blood."

"How do the parents feel about this?"

"Guilty," Maddie answered. "They never told their son about the artificial insemination or the donor sperm, and now the whole situation is blowing up around them."

"Ouch," Tess said, making a face. "Guess they'll have to tell him now. I hope they know a good psychologist because this kid's going to have issues for sure. But I'm sure you'll handle the case with your usual skill and diplomacy."

"I'm not so sure I can remain objective. Tess, this case could be me in ten years. All Jack and I have is a verbal agreement, and if I get pregnant, he could decide years down the road that he wants to play Daddy and put my child through the same kind of hell I went through when my parents divorced."

"Do you really think Jack would do that?"

"I don't know. But I do know that David and Rebecca Stewart never thought Garrett Bates would walk back into their lives and create havoc. She said she'd never have used the man's sperm if she'd known this would happen. I read her deposition and she's absolutely terrified this man is going to try and take away her child."

Maddie reached for a slice of pizza then had second thoughts and put it down.

"I'm not sure under the circumstances that I'm the best person for the job. My gut instinct is to tell Bates exactly which corner of hell he can go to, but wouldn't that go over nicely in court?"

"And if you recuse yourself, you have to tell the judge you got married six weeks ago for the express purpose of getting free sperm and staying in his good graces."

"My father cheated on my mother almost from the day they were married." Maddie's mind burned with powerful memories. "And when I was twelve and he got his secretary pregnant, she demanded he marry her or she'd smear his name all over Nashville. My mother fought to keep the house, and my father bought a new place. Two months after the divorce, my mother married a man ten years younger, and less than two weeks after they said 'I do' he made a pass at me. I told my father and he petitioned the court for custody. That's when the war really started. I was bounced back and forth between them until I was sixteen and told the judge I wanted to go live with my grandmother because my stepmother considered me a rival for my father's emotions and money, and my stepfather didn't understand it wasn't right to lust after me."

"Maddie, I didn't know."

"I went into family law to protect children from what happened to me. And now I might have managed to put a child into the same situation." She laid a protective hand across her abdomen.

"I don't think you have anything to worry about," Tess reassured her. "Consider this. If Jack was such a bad guy, why did Alex ask him to look out for you? Do you really think your former husband would have put you in the hands of someone who didn't have your best interests at heart?"

That had occurred to Maddie, too, but she'd shoved the thought to the back of her mind. "I should have turned Jack down. I should have gone ahead with my original plan and handled whatever consequences came my way. I could go to work for another firm or open my own practice. I—"

"You can second-guess yourself all day, Maddie, but it won't change the fact you've hidden behind your childhood to keep from getting hurt. Now you've stopped hiding and have a second chance at love. I've seen the way Jack looks at you, and I think he really cares."

"*Really cares* and being in love are not the same thing."

Guilt gnawed at her gut, making her regret that third slice of pizza. How could she have let this happen? Lusting after Jack was bad enough, but love wasn't part of the plan. On some level she knew this smelled like a tawdry business transaction. She had to figure out a way to rid herself of the emotions so she could also rid herself of the guilt.

"But *really cares* is a step in the right direction."
Oh, hell.

* * *

Jack sipped from the cup of coffee Millie had just placed on his desk. Even the scalding liquid couldn't shift his thoughts from last night's dream. Maddie had retreated upstairs after their obligatory conception attempt and he'd dreamed about having her in his arms all night, every night.

Over the past five weeks he'd morphed from a bachelor who lived off frozen dinners and Chinese carry-out into a concerned husband who made sure his wife ate a healthy breakfast and carried a nourishing lunch with her to work. Every other night he cooked dinner from some recipe printed off the Internet. He'd wanted to cook every night, but Maddie told him she felt guilty about that and had suggested they alternate.

And then after they'd eaten and cleaned up the kitchen, they'd make small-talk or watch television until Jack asked if it was time for bed.

"Time for bed" was his code phrase for the nightly execution of his plan for getting her pregnant. Most of the time they had sex in his bed, but once they'd done it on his sofa. And last night they'd never made it out of the kitchen.

But whatever the location, he'd lived up to his statement that he'd never have sex with her in the bed she'd shared with Alex.

The past weeks had been…good. Great. Hell, it was fantastic. If this was normal family life, maybe settling down wasn't such a bad idea after all. But he'd already made it clear to Maddie that he wasn't a commitment kind of guy. He'd let himself get carried away a few times during sex, but tried to keep the atmosphere unemotional and casual.

He had one problem though. Keeping the relationship at that level proved to be hard. And he found his body getting harder and harder each time he thought about making love to Maddie. It was bad enough that sex with her was the best ever and he spent hours lusting after her, but now he found himself wondering what it would be like for them to be a family. To have her in his arms each night. Wondering what it would be like to be in love.

He closed his eyes and pinched the bridge of his nose. He didn't have to wonder anymore, because try as he might to deny it, he had fallen in love with his wife. She'd slipped around the wall he'd built around his heart. She'd found the chink in his armor.

"Another long night making babies, boss?" Millie winked and a mischievous grin turned up the corners of her mouth.

"It's none of your damned business." He grabbed a stack of spreadsheets and pretended to study them. "And I'm busy."

"Sure you are," Millie answered, her voice heavy with sarcasm. "I'm so sorry I bothered you." She turned quickly and marched to the doorway.

Jack let the papers drop to the desk. "Come back here, Millie. I'm sorry. I have a lot on my mind right now, especially with the Levernier house."

"Right."

"And I'm bidding on a house for the Braves' new shortstop."

"Sure."

"And—"

Millie moved to stand in front of Jack, placed both palms flat on his desk and leaned toward him. "Why don't you just tell her?"

"Tell who?"

"Maddie. Your wife."

"Tell her what?"

"Tell her you love her." Millie enunciated each word slowly and clearly.

Jack opened his mouth to refute the statement then closed it.

"It's pretty hard to deny the truth, isn't it?"

Jack laid his forehead on the desk and grunted. "Unfortunately, the feeling isn't mutual. Maddie made it clear the marriage was temporary and for convenience only."

"So did you," she countered. "But you think differently now, don't you?"

Jack straightened up and released a long breath. "Why do you always have to be right?"

"Why do *you* always have to be so damn stubborn?"

"So what am I supposed to do? I need something more subtle than just blurting out I love her. That'll spook her for sure."

"You need to do something that shows you're paying attention. Has she mentioned a movie she wanted to see? Something at the art museum? Wait a minute." Millie rushed from the room and returned moments later with the newspaper.

She pulled out one section and opened to the middle page. Jack watched her run a finger down the page, mumbling to herself.

"Here," she said, holding out the paper and tapping the page with her bright red fingernail.

Jack scanned the block of text Millie indicated. "A dancing class?"

"Not any dancing. It's ballroom dancing. Like the TV show."

Jack dropped the paper as if it were on fire. "No way I'm putting on tight pants and waxing my chest."

Millie swatted his arm and rolled her eyes. "Don't be a smart ass. This is a perfect way to let Maddie know you're not just all about the sex. It'll show her a different side of you."

"This isn't that getting–in–touch–with–your–feminine–side stuff, is it?"

Millie threw up her hands and turned on her heel. "Do what you want, Jack, but I'm telling you, you need to let her know how you feel before you lose her."

* * *

Two hours later Jack angled his truck into the parking lot beside Maddie's office and wondered again whether Millie's suggestion was sheer brilliance or a plot doomed to fail. He'd debated calling ahead but decided that dropping in unexpectedly gave him an advantage. She'd be less likely to kick up a fuss in front of her co-workers, and if his luck ran right, he'd be able to propose their dancing date in front of some of her female colleagues.

Ballroom classes would surely impress her friends, and how could she turn him down in front of them without seeming ungrateful or just downright crazy? Add in the sandwiches and fruit he'd purchased at the health food deli and he might just be in the running for Husband of the Year.

The twenty-something receptionist greeted him, and when he introduced himself as Maddie's husband, she reached for the phone to announce his arrival.

"If you'll just aim me toward her office, I'd rather surprise her." Jack flashed the million-watt smile he'd perfected over the years and it did its job.

"I'm not really supposed to let you go anywhere unescorted, but since you're Mrs. Prescott's husband..." She clapped her hand over her mouth and her eyes widened. "Oh my, I'm so sorry. I'm just so used to calling her by that name and—"

Jack smiled again. "Don't you worry about it, uh, Jami," he said, leaning over the desk to read her name from the badge hanging around her neck. "It's an understandable mistake. Now if you could just tell me where her office is, I'd like to take my wife her lunch and tell her about the plans I've made for Friday night." He hefted the bag from the deli and let it swing from his finger.

The young woman giggled and motioned toward the elevator to her left. "Go to the second floor, turn left and her office will be the third one on the left. Her name's on the door. Are you sure you don't want me to call and make sure she's there?"

"I want to surprise her. Promise you won't tell." Jack pursed his lips, placed his index finger against them and made a shushing noise.

During the short elevator ride, Jack mentally rehearsed his speech again. He'd run it past Millie to get a woman's perspective, and he'd repeated it in the truck during the drive downtown.

When the elevator doors swooshed open he found himself face to face with his wife and her best friend.

"Hi, honey," he said, making sure his voice carried to a group of women gathered down the hall. "I brought lunch and thought we could eat in your office." He held the bag in front of him and leaned to give her a peck on the cheek.

"Tess and I were just—"

"I was just going to the sandwich shop at the food court," Tess interrupted. "We'll talk about that new case later. Bye, Jack." Tess stepped into the open elevator and the doors slid shut, leaving Maddie glaring after her.

"Lead on," Jack said, nodding his head in the direction the receptionist had told him.

Maddie cleared her throat and stood her ground.

"I know I should have called first but I thought I'd just surprise you with lunch. And I have another surprise, too." Jack noticed the bevy of women staring and moved closer for another kiss, this time on her lips and lasting long enough to be effective without bordering on a crass public display of affection. When one of the onlookers giggled, Maddie pulled away.

"It's this way," she said and led him into her office.

Jack spread the contents of the bag on the top of her desk. "I wasn't sure if you wanted chicken or turkey so I got one of each. Take your pick."

She selected a sandwich and a ripe, red pear and settled into her desk chair to eat. Jack twisted the cap off a bottle of juice and slid it across to her, then pulled his chair closer to the desk.

* * *

Maddie chewed thoughtfully, racking her brain for a clue to Jack's spontaneous lunch appearance but could think of none. There was no way he could know about the new case she'd been agonizing over, and she certainly wasn't going to tell him and plant any ideas in his head.

"So what's the other surprise?"

"I signed us up for a dancing class. I didn't think you had anything else scheduled and it looked like fun. It's for couples who want to take a test drive before they sign up for a whole series of classes. You said one time you'd like to take ballroom classes and I saw this and…" Jack shrugged, almost embarrassed, and dumped the rest of his potato chips onto the sandwich wrapper. "I thought it might be nice to have a real date since we never really dated before we got married."

"We did so. We went to that Italian restaurant and…and… I can't remember exact dates and places, but we did."

"I'll give you the night at Little Sicily, but that's it. We didn't date, Maddie. We had interviews. You had lists of the pros and cons of my being a sperm donor and then a list about getting married. I felt like I was applying for a job."

He had been, in a manner of speaking. At the time, she'd only been concerned with the logistics of her monthly cycle and getting him into a room at the fertility clinic at the proper time. But after almost six weeks of marriage everything had changed, especially since they'd put Jack's new plan into play.

She watched a muscle in his jaw twitch, and her emotions raced because she knew she'd made him mad. He'd brought her lunch and remembered a comment she'd made at the Fire and Ice ball. How many times had she heard co-workers complain their husbands and boyfriends never listened to them?

And what would be so bad about being in Jack's arms on a dance floor? She'd never admit it, especially not to Jack, but he hadn't been the only one aroused by their dance that night. She'd felt a shockwave of desire course through her the moment he pulled her against his body.

"When's the class?" she asked, steering the conversation away from the issue of dates.

"It's tonight at six on the Tech campus and lasts an hour. I thought maybe we could go to the class and then swing by the Varsity for hot dogs before we head home and, well, you know."

"Yeah." *Oh, how I know.*

You know meant going downstairs for sex even though they had passed day ten of Jack's plan to get her pregnant. She had rationalized her continuing visits to Jack's bed with the thought that a few extra days would improve the odds of conception. On the nights she didn't fall asleep in his arms, she returned to her bedroom wrapped in Jack's bathrobe or wearing one of his t-shirts that hung to her knees and carried his scent.

Most nights she never bothered to change, and on those nights she never slept well. Too many emotions swirled through her head to allow sleep, and she would spend the following day fighting fatigue at work. Today had been one of those days. Add in the new case and no wonder she was a wreck.

Maybe she should just forget her rule and stay in Jack's bed every night. Then she'd be able to sleep soundly and perform at work.

"So is it a date?" Jack's eager expression reminded her of a boy outside a candy store window.

She took in a deep breath and exhaled slowly, hoping to calm her jittery nerves. "It's a date."

* * *

"George Bernard Shaw defined dancing as the vertical expression of a horizontal desire legalized by music. The tango is the dance of love and passion. You'll be in closed position, and ladies, you need to tuck your right hip bone into the pocket of your partner's right hip."

The female half of the instructing duo moved around the room coaxing couples into the correct stance while her partner readied the music. After the grace of the waltz and the exuberance of the swing, Maddie recognized that the tango was going to move things in an entirely different direction both in terms of dancing and her body's response to Jack's proximity.

"I believe this one's my favorite," Jack said against her lips as he tugged her a bit closer. "And after we learn the vertical version, we'll do the horizontal one when we get home." He brushed his lips across her forehead as he moved back into proper dance position. "Maybe we'll get those hot dogs to go, huh?"

With their hips touching and his hand on her back, every nerve ending in Maddie's body accelerated to high alert. Once the music started and Jack led her around the room, concentrating on the pattern of dance steps kept her mind off Jack's promise of what lay in store for her.

When the instructor announced the end of class, Maddie grabbed her purse and jacket in a rush, which was ridiculous since they'd already completed the ten days of Plan B. Any sex they had now would be purely recreational since the window for procreation had passed. And wasn't that exactly what she *didn't* want?

"What do you want to eat?" Jack asked. "A couple of chili slaw dogs? I promise I won't eat any onions tonight."

"Anxious for that horizontal tango, are you?" Maddie tried and failed to keep her irritation at bay.

Jack grinned devilishly and Maddie felt her nerve endings burn hotter. The man definitely got under her skin, only now it was more from desire than annoyance. The wicked sense of humor she'd initially found so infuriating now turned her on.

"I need to eat now, Jack." Her stomach growled as if on cue.

"Are you okay?" Jack traced his finger along her jaw, fanning the flames of desire.

"I'm fine. It's been a long day," she lied, knowing full well the day hadn't been any longer than usual. Somehow she had to figure out how to deal with the attraction she felt for Jack. He was enjoying their time in bed knowing there were no strings attached while her heart became more attached by the day.

In her law practice she'd seen too many marriages gone sour, and she had experienced the effects of divorce firsthand. She needed to rein in her emotions before she put herself in a position to be hurt.

"I'll walk you to your car and then follow you to the Varsity in my truck. Unless you'd rather go somewhere else?" His voice carried a tone she couldn't quite make out. Was he angry she'd derailed his plans or simply concerned about her well-being?

"The Varsity is fine." The sooner they ate, the sooner she could get home and escape to her bedroom for a long, hot bath and a mental dressing down for allowing herself to be swayed by the man's good looks and charm.

Once they'd reached the restaurant, Jack placed their order and found a booth amidst the hordes of college students who packed the place each night.

"Here you go," he said. "We need to make sure you get plenty of protein."

Maddie eyed the overflowing tray in front of her. "How many of these are for me?" She counted six hot dogs on the tray and wondered if it were some sort of phallic display of power.

"You can have as many wieners as you want." He winked and Maddie knew her hunch was correct. "I got you a milkshake, too. Calcium, you know." He slid a large cup in front of her and jabbed a straw into the thick, chocolate mixture.

"Are you trying to get me fat?"

"No, I'm trying to get you pregnant."

"Keep your voice down." She glanced around cautiously.

"There are eight hundred people in here talking at once. Nobody's going to hear me. And besides, couples get pregnant every day. It's not an unmentionable topic anymore."

"Why did you take me to the class tonight?" she asked, deliberately changing the subject.

"Because I thought you might enjoy it. I certainly did."

"Why did you keep trying when I didn't get pregnant the first time? I gave you an easy out."

"What's with the twenty questions? This is starting to feel like another of your interviews instead of the date it was supposed to be."

Jack bit the end off a hot dog and chewed slowly, his unwavering gaze pinned on her.

"Answer the damn question," Maddie ground out between clenched teeth.

Jack nodded toward the table. "Eat the damn food."

"You are the most annoying man." Maddie polished off an entire hot dog in five bites and washed it down with the milkshake. "Satisfied?"

"Yeah, just don't complain to me when you have indigestion in the middle of the night."

"Now answer the question. Why didn't you take the easy way out?"

"Because a very important man in my life taught me that nothing worth having was ever simple, and that most things in life are difficult before they are easy."

"He was probably talking about bowling or learning to ride a bike."

Jack swirled the straw in his milkshake, then pushed the cup aside. "Doesn't matter what it is. The easy way isn't always what's best for you. I made a promise, first to Alex and then to you. And a promise is a promise and a deal is a deal. If you want to break it, go right ahead. But don't *ever* think that I'm not a man of my word."

They ate the rest of their meal in silence, or as much silence as you could have in the middle of eight hundred people. Maddie sneaked glances at Jack when she thought he wasn't looking. Maybe all the gossip about him had been wrong. She'd readily believed everything she'd overheard at office parties and the cookouts Alex would organize in their backyard. But why would Alex have picked Jack to look out for her if he'd been a notorious playboy?

Jack himself had confessed his bad boy background to her. But not once during the time they'd been married and living together had he been anything but honest and forthcoming. He'd seemed almost embarrassed when she told him she knew about the bone marrow donation.

She'd goaded him on several occasions and he'd maintained his cool. Her whole line of questioning tonight could be construed as picking a fight. Perhaps a fight to drive him away so she didn't have to deal with the fact she'd fallen in love with a man who would never love her back?

"You finished?" Jack wadded food wrappers and napkins into a ball as he moved outside the booth.

Maddie could see the tension in his jaw—tension she'd caused. She nodded and followed as he led the way to her car. He opened the door, stepped aside and let her slide behind the wheel. He leaned into the open doorway, his bulk blocking the street light and darkening the car's interior.

"Drive carefully and lock your doors."

Maddie nodded again and twisted the key in the ignition after he closed the door and walked toward his truck. The drive home took less than ten minutes and as soon as she'd parked the car and lowered the garage door, she entered the house and reset the security system. She dropped her purse on the kitchen desk, shrugged out of her suit jacket and hurried to her bedroom. She never closed the door because Jack had made it clear he'd never enter without an invitation.

Ten minutes later, she heard the alarm system beep and knew Jack was home. As she cleaned her face, she listened for Jack to run through his nightly routine before heading downstairs—filling the coffee maker for the next morning, checking the doors to make sure they were locked, tuning in to the local television station for the weather forecast. Instead she heard muffled music from below and realized he'd gone straight downstairs.

Maddie glanced at the bedside clock and understood. Though their awkward dinner had seemed to last an eternity, it was only eight-thirty. She changed into a pair of cotton pajamas and matching robe, tying the belt tightly around her waist. She paused when the knot was done and glanced down where her hands rested against her abdomen.

What if she'd become pregnant during this cycle? Was she already carrying Jack's child? Would he be as involved in her pregnancy as he'd been in the conception process? Or would he consider his job done and fade into the background? That would be the easy path for him to follow, except now she knew his attitude toward the easy way out.

Three hours later, tired of staring at the clock, she wandered to the den and began thumbing through a stack of law journals, hoping to be bored to sleep. Thirty wide-awake minutes later she heard the door from the basement open and watched as Jack walked into the kitchen wearing only a pair of wrinkled boxers. His hair stuck out at odd angles as if he'd just awakened from a restless sleep.

He flipped the wall switch and the overhead light flashed on. He squinted against the brightness and when he finally opened his eyes, he stared directly at her across the two rooms.

"I didn't know you were still awake," he mumbled sleepily. "I ran out of milk and thought I'd…" He gestured toward the refrigerator. "I'll just go back down."

While he steadied himself against the counter dividing the rooms, Maddie laid the magazine aside and walked to the opposite side of the counter. She didn't trust herself to get any closer because she might be tempted to smooth his hair or pour him that glass of milk because he looked mighty tempting right now.

"Don't go," she whispered. "I need to…to…apologize. I'm sorry for the way I acted earlier. You surprised me with lunch, took me dancing and treated me to your favorite place to eat, and I behaved like a petulant child."

"Don't worry about it. I was an ass."

"Only because I provoked you." Maddie blinked as tears gathered in her eyes. "I just have all these confusing feelings. We have this complicated marriage where I live upstairs and you live downstairs like the hired help. We have sex in your bed and then I slip out after you've gone to sleep and go back to my bedroom. I'm not really your wife—"

"Legally, you are."

"That's what this whole arrangement is about. Legalities. But if I'm your wife, why do I feel like a whore?"

Jack was beside her before she could say another word and he pulled her close. "Don't ever say that again. Don't ever feel that way," he said as he wiped away her tears. "Would a man treat a whore like this?" he asked as he brushed his lips gently against hers. "Or this?" he continued, trailing a finger down her body, careful to avoid her breasts. "Or this?"

Jack released her and stepped back, his hands fisted tightly at his side. Maddie saw his erection tenting the front of his boxers. Without another word, he turned and walked back to the stairway leading to the basement.

"No man would walk away from a bought-and-paid-for woman. Goodnight, Maddie." He closed the door behind him and left her standing alone and aroused.

And completely in love.

Eleven

Maddie stared at the paraphernalia scattered around her bathroom. She'd left work at lunch and bought pregnancy tests at a drugstore. Boxes and papers were spread all over, nearly as scattered as her thoughts. But her main focus was the three stick-like objects by the sink. One by one she examined them.

A plus sign, two lines and finally the word *PREGNANT* confirmed what she'd suspected for days.

She was going to have a baby.

Her baby.

Jack's baby.

At some point she'd fallen in love with Jack. She couldn't believe it had happened. Was it when he'd agreed to debase himself with a magazine and a plastic specimen cup? When he put on a suit and tie and said "I do" to save the job she cared so much about? Or was it when he insisted she enjoy the sex?

When he put on a public performance at the Fire and Ice ball to prove they were happily wed, her world had shifted as well as her view of the man. And the kiss—that kiss was not just a show for everyone around them. It was the real thing, and she had kissed right back, just as real, just as filled with passion.

How would he feel now that sperm and egg had collided and in nine months she'd have a baby? Would the baby look like him and be a reminder? She'd promised him that there was no expectation on her part, but if he saw a baby boy who had his same blue eyes and dimples, would he decide the promise was null and void?

She had become used to life alone after Alex died. She'd made the initial pregnancy decision alone and had been perfectly content to raise a child alone. After all, living in a loving, single-parent family would be far better than living in the hell she had.

But now she was used to life with Jack. She was used to the sound of his voice around the house, the sight of him lounging on the sofa, the smell of his aftershave when he was close to her. And she'd gotten very used to being in his bed. Could she go back to the aloneness again?

If it meant not having to worry about her child being used as the rope in a parental tug of war, then yes.

But could she kick Jack out of her heart?

She would have to.

Living with one heartbreak would be easier than living with three hundred sixty-five heartbreaks a year if she stayed with a man who didn't love her. It would be a daily reminder of being with a parent who didn't love her either.

She scooped the test sticks and packaging off the counter and into the wastebasket. Then, as an afterthought, she pulled one back out thinking she should save it as a souvenir for the baby book. She glanced down to see which one she'd grabbed. The word *PREGNANT* greeted her again.

Pregnant with Jack's baby. Pregnant by a man who wasn't a commitment kind of guy. How had she let herself fall in love with him, and why did she want him now?

She stuffed the test stick into the nightstand drawer and then sat on the edge of the bed, pressing her hand to her abdomen. A new, fragile life rested there. A life created by a man who had made her feel alive again after so many months of living in the dark. He'd also awakened her sexually and she was sure the memories of their nights together were driving her emotions now.

She wanted him, but she knew what she wanted wasn't necessarily what was best. And what was best right now was to put Jack at a distance so she could think rationally and devise a plan of action.

Maddie pulled the phone from the nightstand and began to dial Tess's number. Perhaps she could stay with her friend until she figured out how to extricate Jack from her life. She hesitated, though, knowing Tess's apartment would be the first place Jack looked if he came home and found her gone.

Calling Millie was out of the question, too. She and Jack were as thick as thieves, and Millie wouldn't keep her secret. Her only option was to get out of Atlanta for a while until she decided what course of action to take. Then she could call Tess and see what kind of legal magic the two of them could work.

When they'd signed their prenuptial agreement and shook hands on their parental agreement prior to the wedding, Maddie hadn't worried that Jack might renege. She may have lost her heart, but she had no indication the feelings were mutual. He'd made love to her with incredible passion and caring, but was it any more than pure pleasure for him? Once the two a.m. feedings and dirty diapers came along, he would decide it was time to call it quits just as they'd agreed.

We'll know when the time is right, he'd said. And it was right at this moment. She had her own money, a good job and the means to support herself and a child more than comfortably.

She just had to figure out how to stop leaning on Jack for emotional support. If she could do that—*when* she did that, she corrected—life would go back to her original plan.

She pulled a suitcase from the closet and filled it with clothing to last a few days. She'd just get in the car and drive north until...

Until she reached the road that led to Pleasant Junction, Cedar Gap and Jack's cabin. He would never think to look for her there. She'd have to get a key from Charlotte Tanner since she had no clue if Jack had one downstairs. During the drive she could concoct some story to convince Mrs. Tanner that her visit was purely innocuous and not that she was on the lam.

Charlotte was special to Jack, though Maddie didn't know why. The last thing she wanted was to damage their friendship with her personal situation.

She locked the house and tossed the suitcase in the trunk. Once he knew the situation, Jack would understand. He would forgive her the deception and stealthy escape. She just had to forgive herself for falling in love with him.

* * *

"Maddie?" Jack stepped into her bedroom and called to her. The empty bay in the garage had puzzled him, but he knew she and Tess sometimes went shopping or to dinner after work. The dark house was easily explainable as well, though she usually left a note. There was none unless he'd just missed it.

When he saw the half-opened drawer on her dresser and the clothes she'd worn to work in a heap on her bed, panic began to rise in his throat. Maddie was neat to a fault—a place for everything and everything in its place. No way she'd leave dirty clothes lying around unless there was an emergency of some sort.

But what was the emergency? She was estranged from her parents, but he doubted she'd be so callous to ignore a real crisis involving one of them.

He tried her cell phone and left a message on her voice mail then made his way to her bathroom, which was uncharacteristically messy. A damp towel lay wadded in a corner and the wastebasket sat on the counter. Without thinking he picked up the towel and hung it neatly across the metal rod. Then he grabbed the wastebasket and leaned to put it back in place.

A brightly colored box in the bottom of the container captured his attention and he fished it out. Underneath it were two other boxes, each labeled Pregnancy Test.

He'd lost track of the days after they'd begun sleeping together every night and making love into the wee hours. He mentally calculated and his gut clenched. Had she used a series of pregnancy tests and received the same repeated negative result? No wonder she wasn't home. She'd probably run to Tess's for comfort, though he wondered why she wouldn't come to him. They'd shared so much over the last weeks. Surely she knew he would understand.

Truth be told, he would be disappointed, too. Somewhere along the way, his promise had turned into something a whole lot more. More than mere obligation and a hell of a lot more than saving her job.

She'd crawled under his skin and into his heart, and he wanted to be there for her to share the disappointment of this most recent failed pregnancy attempt.

He poured the contents of the can onto the counter to see just how many times she had tried to make the result change from negative to positive, from bad to good, and he found two test sticks. He picked one up and glanced at the result window, then checked the instructions on the packaging.

His jaw clenched when he saw a plus sign, and then he turned the second stick over and saw another positive result. He rummaged through the trash on the counter. The third test stick wasn't there, but he'd bet everything he owned it was positive, too.

Maddie was pregnant. The plan had worked—the nights together in his bed, the long shower they'd taken together, the afternoon she'd stopped by his office and they'd used the drafting table for something it had never been designed for. One of those times they'd made love had succeeded.

Seeing the positive results, he knew it meant "yes" for a baby. But something in his heart cracked and he realized he'd broken his own rule and fallen in love with this disarming woman. He'd fallen hard and what had started as a safe, convenient marriage with them merely coexisting under the same roof had turned into a lot more. He'd never expected anything from their marriage or from her, and he knew she shared the sentiment.

She was probably as scared over a positive result as she would have been disappointed over a negative one. But why leave? Why not stay and let him assure her that everything would work out? Hell, he knew the answer. She didn't feel the same way he did. She had her baby and now his role was over.

But he still needed to protect her until he was sure her pregnancy was a healthy one. Or maybe until the baby was safely born. Or he could stay until the baby slept through the night, or why not just stay until it left for college and he had her all to himself again. Because Jack wasn't going to be satisfied with anything less than happily ever after with his wife—his wife in every legal and emotional sense of the word.

He kept out one of the test sticks and brushed the remaining trash back into the wastebasket. Pulling his cell phone from the holder on his belt, he dialed Tess then paused before he hit the call button.

He'd confront Maddie at Tess's house and convince her to come back home. He'd tell her how excited he was that Plan B had worked. And once she was convinced of that, he'd convince her to stay with him for the rest of his life.

* * *

"I don't know where she is, Jack," Tess insisted, peering around her barely open front door. "And if you don't mind, I have *company* and I'd like to get back to them."

Jack braced one hand against the door frame and shoved the door with the other. "I want to see her, Tess. I know what's going on so don't keep me from her."

The door swung wide and Jack saw a man stretched out on the sofa, his arm thrown across his eyes.

"Satisfied?" Tess stepped into the open walkway outside her apartment and pulled the door shut behind her. "She isn't here, but you're beginning to scare me. What is it you know that would make you think she'd come over here?"

Jack pulled the test stick from his pocket and held it out toward her. "She's pregnant. Pregnant with my baby and I'll be damned if I let her run away and leave another fatherless child in the wake."

"Is that the only reason?" Tess sent him a piercing look and he backed up a step. "Are you merely wanting to keep her baby from being labeled as illegitimate, because I can assure you it's not a stigma anymore. Lots of single women have babies every day for one reason or another and society doesn't point a finger like it once did."

"I don't care about society. I know what it's like to have those fingers pointing at you and dammit, the woman I love isn't going to put my child through that."

Tess crossed her arms across her chest and leaned against the door. "I thought as much," she said. "You care about what people think about the baby, but more importantly, you love the baby's mother. Have you told her?"

"Oh, God." His face blanched. "Why didn't I tell her before I put her in a position to wonder about it, and obviously decide I didn't care?" He slapped a hand against the brick wall in frustration. "You have to help me find her. Are you sure she didn't leave you a message or something and let you know where she was going?"

"I'm sure," Tess said. "But you've been living with her for a while. Think. If you were upset about something and needed to escape, where would you go?"

Twelve

Gravel crunched under the tires as Maddie passed the Pair-o-Dice
sign and drove onto Charlotte's property. She'd meant to ask Jack
about the meaning of the sign, but somewhere between pre-sex
jitters and post-sex contentment she forgot. She just hoped the older
woman still had a key to the cabin.

If she didn't, perhaps Maddie could scavenge around the cabin
and find one hidden under a rock or in a tree stump. Of course, there
was the alarm system he'd had installed and she had no clue about
the security code to disarm it even if she could get the door unlocked.
She just had to hope Charlotte had a key and the code was the same
one she had given the installer.

Rummaging through Jack's things downstairs to look for them
had never been an option. Though she might try to find a way around
his privacy, she'd never deliberately invade it.

Instead, Maddie had used the driving time to come up with a
plausible reason for her to visit the cabin alone, should Charlotte ask.
Once she'd figured that out, the whole idea of being pregnant took
over, and she'd begun making a mental to-do list for the coming
weeks and months. She needed to see her doctor and start prenatal
care. She had to find a pediatrician and a good nanny. The corner
bedroom upstairs would make a wonderful nursery, but it needed a
fresh coat of paint. Until she learned the baby's gender, though,
she'd hold off on any decorating and furniture purchases.

She'd need to buy a new car—one more child-friendly than her
two-door coupe. And a car seat and stroller and a cradle to keep
beside her bed in the early weeks. As the mental list grew, so did
Maddie's anxiety level. The drive, which should have taken an hour,
took twice that long. She'd had to stop twice because her vision
became too blurred by tears to drive safely.

By the time she reached the Tanner place, her nerves were
stretched as taut as the horsehair on a violin bow. She hoped she
could hold her emotions in check long enough to find a way to get in
the cabin, and once there, she could fall apart. After a good cry she
could begin to sort things out and figure out how to break the news
to Jack.

Maddie braked to a stop where the gravel drive ended. On the previous visit, she hadn't noticed the flowerbeds filled with brilliant blossoms or the wooden garden swing in the shade of a massive maple tree. Her mind had been wrapped around one thing only that day.

She turned off the ignition, grabbed her purse and swung the car door open. Squaring her shoulders and steeling her nerves, she picked her way along a stone path then climbed the four steps to the porch. Without a phone number, Maddie hadn't been able to call ahead.

She rapped her knuckles against the heavy wooden door, praying Charlotte was home. If she wasn't, Maddie would rely on her backup plan—a hotel room on the main highway. A hotel room would provide lodging, but Maddie needed some place where she could walk off her anxiety and figure out her plan of action. The cabin was perfect.

She had raised her hand to knock again and the door swung open.

"Maddie? What a nice surprise? Come in, dear." Charlotte looked past her toward the car. "Is Jack with you?"

Maddie shook her head. "I came by myself. Jack's so busy with a big project and I've been bogged down at work and wanted a couple days of fresh air and quiet. One of my girlfriends is going to drive up tomorrow morning and join me." Maddie crossed her fingers behind her back. "But I was in a hurry to leave and got halfway here and realized I forgot to bring the key and write down the alarm code so…"

"I'll get the spare key for you and write down the code," Charlotte began. "Come in, dear."

Maddie stepped inside, and just as Charlotte left, her cell phone vibrated in her pocket. A quick glance at the screen indicated Jack's number, and she let the call roll to voice mail.

Maddie stiffened her resolve, shoved the phone back in her pocket and studied her surroundings.

She guessed this was the den. The walls were a neutral shade of beige but the room had been decorated with plenty of color. The burgundy leather sofa was complimented by a wingback chair upholstered in a multi-colored striped fabric. Two ottomans in a tapestry print sat in front of a stone fireplace. A large painting of a field of poppies hung over an oak mantel, and throw pillows in various fabrics lined up like soldiers in a window seat with a panoramic view of the mountains. Wood floors like the ones in Jack's cabin gleamed around the edges of a large area rug in tan and muted reds.

This house was a home filled with warmth and love. A home that invited a visitor to come in and relax. A home like Maddie wanted for her child.

She moved to examine a wall unit that housed a television, an eclectic assortment of books and a collection of photographs, one of which caught her interest. Maddie picked up a picture of a much younger Alex and an older man standing side-by-side with brilliant autumn foliage in the background.

"That was taken under the big maple in the front. The one with the swing under it," Charlotte said, startling Maddie from her thoughts. "We'd just bought this property."

"You knew Alex?"

Charlotte took the photo and rubbed her finger down the side of the wooden frame.

"We hired him and Jack to build our dream home."

Maddie stomach clenched. If Charlotte had known Alex, perhaps she also knew how recently Alex had died and how quickly Maddie had married his best friend. "They certainly did a great job because it's definitely a dream."

"But this isn't the home Edmond and I originally planned. Didn't Jack tell you about it when you were here before?"

"The uh...subject never came up." She and Jack had been focused on one thing only, and it wasn't stories about past clients. "But I did wonder about the name on the sign by the gate."

"Edmond was involved in developing the gambling industry on the Gulf Coast back in the nineties."

Maddie made the connection to the sign by the gate and nodded as her phone vibrated once more. Once more she ignored it.

"When he retired he wanted to move away from the shore. Away from the crowds and heat and hurricanes. We found this piece of property, bought it and hired an architect to design the home we'd live in forever. And that autumn day, we signed the contract with Alex to build it." She tapped the frame's glass with her fingernail and handed the photo to Maddie.

"Two weeks before we were scheduled to break ground, Edmond had a massive heart attack and died. We'd sold our house in Biloxi, put most of our things in storage and were living in a rented condo." Charlotte stared blankly out the window. "I remember driving back up here after the funeral and feeling so cold and alone. The trees were bare and the ground was frozen. The place didn't look much like paradise to me."

"I'm so sorry," Maddie said, carefully replacing the photo. She understood losing a spouse and knew all too well that cold and alone feeling.

"I telephoned Alex's office to see what was required to break our contract and Jack answered the phone. He told me he'd have Alex call me. Three days later, Jack showed up at my door with a plan. He bought the land from me, built this smaller home and gave me a lifetime lease on it. Then he remodeled that old dairy barn into a cabin for himself."

Charlotte held out a scrap of blue paper and a single key on a piece of braided leather. "I hope you get what you came for, dear. If you need anything, just call. My number is on a list by the kitchen phone."

Maddie's phone vibrated a third time and for the third time she ignored it.

Maddie took the key in one hand and grabbed for the slip of paper with the other. But Charlotte held on tight.

"If that's Jack calling, you may as well answer because that boy won't give up. I don't know what kind of problem made you run up here, but don't doubt for a minute that when Jack wants something he doesn't stop until he gets it. And my dear, he wants you."

"No..." Maddie began and shook her head.

"I think you love him very much, too."

Maddie chewed her lower lip to keep it from quivering and giving away the true state of her emotions.

"Edmond and I were married for forty-four years, so I know a thing or two about love and marriage." Charlotte released the paper. "Don't close any doors or burn any bridges. No matter how dark the night is, there's light when the sun rises, and things appear much differently in the light."

Maddie tucked the key and paper in her pocket, thanked Charlotte and hastily returned to her car. She just wanted to reach the cabin, get inside and curl up in a ball in the dark to process the situation.

She pulled her car under the carport and made certain she could get into the house before retrieving her suitcase from the trunk. Jack kept basic staple items in the pantry, and she'd picked up a deli sandwich and several bottles of juice before she'd left the main highway. Tomorrow she could take stock of the supplies on hand and venture out for more food if necessary.

She pulled her wheeled bag through the living area toward the bedroom and the cabin closed in around her. Every sight and smell reminded her of the first time she and Jack had made love. Had tried to make a baby. Then it had just been sex. But now?

The last few weeks had been amazing and she'd done exactly what she'd had promised herself she wouldn't do. She'd fallen in love with Jack. Fallen in love with her husband and it terrified her.

Everyone presumed they had a fairy tale marriage. She wished it was. She longed for it, but she had to accept that Jack would never love her, regardless of what Charlotte said. Maddie knew him. It wasn't part of the bargain. She had to resign herself to making life as wonderful as possible for her little family of two.

After stowing the suitcase in the bedroom and having her emotions derailed again by the sight of the big bed, she returned to the living room and pulled the drapes back. The surrounding trees cast long shadows as the sun dropped lower in the horizon behind the cabin. The cloudless sky would fill with stars once the sun disappeared completely.

If she was lucky, maybe she could see the first star and make a wish—a wish for an easy pregnancy and a healthy baby. A wish that when she broke the news to Jack and then ended their relationship in the next breath, her own heart wouldn't shatter into a thousand tiny pieces.

* * *

Once Jack was thoroughly convinced Tess knew nothing about Maddie's whereabouts, he played her question over and over in his head on the drive back home.

Where would she go?

She had friends but none he thought were close enough to house his runaway wife. Her parents still lived in Nashville but she'd never run there. The grandmother who raised her and gave her away at her marriage to Alex had died a year after the wedding. If she had run to Millie, he'd have known about it by now. Millie had made it clear he could expect a lynching if he hurt Maddie.

If she was holed up in a hotel, he'd never find her. The metro Atlanta area had a hotel on every corner. Though he didn't expect success, he dialed the Georgian Terrace, where he'd spent his honeymoon night sleeping on a sofa, and asked to be connected to Mrs. Worth's room. They had no one by the name of Worth, Prescott or her maiden name, Yates.

When he'd exhausted all possibilities and still had not found her, he realized just how little he really knew about his wife.

His *wife*.

And now the mother of his child.

"Where the hell are you, woman?" he muttered as he thumbed the button on his cell phone to dial her for the third time. Maybe she had someone monitoring the house and if he left she'd come back.

How desperate can you get, Worth? But at this stage he'd try anything. He could put things on hold at the office for a few days and drive to the cabin. Sitting on the deck watching the sunrise might help him decide what to do about his impending fatherhood.

The cabin.

Jack scrolled through the contact list on his phone and dialed Charlotte. "Is she there?" he blurted out before the woman could even say hello.

"Is who where?"

Bingo. The pause before she answered told him what he needed to know. He drew in a huge breath and blew it out in relief.

"Thank you, Charlotte. That's all the answer I need. I'll be at the cabin in an hour or so."

"Come to my house first, Jack." Charlotte hesitated again briefly before continuing. "I think you need to wait until morning to talk with Maddie. You can stay in my guest room tonight."

"Why? Is something wrong with her? I mean physically?" Jack knew from the books he'd read that pregnant women weren't frail objects needing to be encased in bubble wrap. But Maddie had a brand new life growing inside her, and even under the best circumstances, things could go wrong.

"She's exhausted from the drive and emotionally on the edge. I don't know what's going on between you two, and it's none of my business. But you need to tread carefully."

Jack debated telling Charlotte about the positive pregnancy tests he'd found but held back. He'd accept her offer of the guest room and see just how much she already knew before potentially opening Pandora's Box.

Jack ended the call, packed a change of clothes and left a trail of rubber on the pavement in his hurry to get out of town.

Settle down.

The last thing he needed was a ticket for speeding or reckless driving. Charlotte's non-answer had confirmed his hunch. He'd give Maddie the night to work through whatever had caused her to disappear, and then they'd talk.

He reached to the passenger seat of his truck and touched the manila envelope he hoped was his ticket to setting things straight. Surely Maddie would hear him out and return home once he pled his case.

Fifteen minutes later he merged onto the Georgia 400, set the cruise control and tried again to understand why Maddie had bolted when she'd gotten what she wanted. He'd have been the more likely candidate for a quick escape, only he no longer felt the need to avoid commitments. Or more specifically, a single commitment to a particular woman.

His initial response to Maddie had been lust, and even at that, the slide into lust had been gradual. But once the momentum began, a crash landing into love was fast and inevitable. He'd never been so affected by a woman. Why did this one with legs that went on forever and a voice that reminded him of lazy afternoons in bed have him tied in knots?

Jack hadn't simply fallen for Maddie. He'd walked right up to the edge, jumped off and plummeted over the side. And damn if it hadn't felt good.

Fifty-five minutes later his truck tripped the motion lights outside Charlotte's home and she stepped onto the front porch.

"I have hot coffee ready for you," she said and wrapped him in a hug. "Cookies, too, if you're hungry."

"You know I have a weakness when it comes to your cookies. You don't play fair at all." He held the door open and followed her inside. The aroma of sugar and chocolate welcomed him, and after stowing his bag in the guest room, he joined Charlotte at her kitchen table.

They made small talk while he downed the coffee and when nothing but crumbs remained from the half-dozen chocolate chip cookies she'd put on a china plate, Jack had run out of excuses not to talk about Maddie.

"How did you know she was at the cabin?" Jack asked, brushing cookie crumbs into a pile.

"She came here to get the key and alarm code. I'm surprised your wife didn't know where to find it."

Jack winced slightly at the emphasis on the word wife and wondered how much Charlotte knew about his and Maddie's unconventional marriage. When he'd visited the previous month, he'd told Charlotte the same story he told everyone—they fell in love, had a small, quiet wedding, no big deal.

"Guess I forgot to show her."

"I think you've forgotten to show her a lot of things." Her chair scraped against the tile floor as she pushed away from the table, gathered the plates and cups and set them in the sink.

Jack waited for the other shoe to drop.

"It's been a long day and I am going to sleep now. Stay up as long as you like." She paused in the doorway leading to the living room. "There's a homemade coffee cake by the coffee maker in case you want to earn brownie points tomorrow morning. I can't assure you how successful you'll be, but if I were you, I'd give it a try."

Jack scrubbed a hand across his nape. "I think it's going to take more than coffee cake and my charming personality to help me now. I've messed everything up and now she's—" Jack bit back the word, unsure of how much Charlotte knew.

"She's worried and she's scared," Charlotte replied. "But she's also in love with you."

"I wish I could believe you, but if she's so in love, why did she run away?"

"That's what the two of you are going to have to work out. The good Lord gave you two ears and one mouth, so use them in that proportion. Listen to her, Jack, and listen to your own heart. You've built a wall around it and kept everyone out. Somehow that woman sneaked through and I believe the thought of anybody actually loving you scares you to death. But what scares you more is letting yourself love her."

Jack opened his mouth to disagree then realized Charlotte was right. Loving and being loved was a whole new experience for him. Scary as it was, he had to remember that now there were more than two people in the relationship. He and Maddie had created a child, and if what Charlotte said was true, this child could grow up in a loving home with two parents who loved it and loved each other.

Take care of her, Jack. Promise me.

Now he had to take care of *them.*

The next morning, Jack walked the half-mile to the cabin shortly after eight and waited until he saw signs of life inside before he approached. He climbed the steps to the deck and knocked on the glass door. He knew better than to just walk in. He wanted Maddie to feel safe, in control and like she had choices, and walking in unannounced would leave her feeling just the opposite.

He saw the look of surprise in her eyes when she saw him through the door, and he wouldn't have blamed her if she'd bolted the door and pulled the drapes shut. To his relief, she opened the door though she said nothing.

"Charlotte sent coffee cake," he said, holding out the foil-wrapped loaf in one hand. In the other hand he held the manila envelope. He was counting on its contents along with the speech he'd spent half the night rehearsing to help him plead his case.

Maddie remained silent as she took his offering and stepped aside to let him enter. Her eyes were red-rimmed and her disheveled clothes led him to believe she'd slept in them.

They stared awkwardly at each other and Jack was determined to follow Charlotte's advice to listen twice as much as he talked. He'd let Maddie speak her mind, yell, scream and cry, but he intended to state his case before he left.

He'd been awake half the night remembering the two months since they'd said "I do." He'd convinced himself he could enter into a short-term marriage in order to keep his promise to Alex, but somewhere along the way, the promise faded into the background and the marriage had begun to seem real.

"What's in the envelope?" she asked, setting the cake on the dining table.

Jack had hoped to hold off revealing its contents until after they'd had a chance to at least exchange a few pleasantries. Now she'd called his hand and he wouldn't insult her intelligence by trying to avoid the question.

He reached inside, pulled out the pregnancy test he'd retrieved from her bathroom and held it up. Her eyes widened and she spread her hand protectively across her abdomen.

"My plan worked," he said, his voice even and emotionless.

Maddie squared her shoulders and her chin lifted. "Yes, it did. And now you've done your job and it's time for us to go back to life like it was before."

"Before what?" he asked, taking a step closer. "Before Alex died? Before I saved your job?"

"That's low and you know it. You know exactly what I mean. It's time to call it quits."

"And what do we tell folks when we return the wedding gifts?"

"We'll just tell them it didn't work out—"

"—and that I walked out and left you with a bun in the oven? No thanks," he replied sharply. "That's not the message I want to send to the world. Or to my child."

"You're not walking out on me. You were never *in* me."

Jack waved the test stick at her. "Oh, but this says I was."

"You know what I mean."

He reached in the envelope and pulled out the remainder of the contents. "If you're talking about this arrangement—"

"I'm un-arranging it. You can move your stuff out of my basement and get back to your life."

Jack thumbed through the papers and held up one document. "This is our prenup, and it's not what bothers me. What's yours is yours, regardless. But *this* is another matter." He held up another sheaf of papers. "This is our unofficial handshake contract that says I'm not responsible for any child that might result from our marriage."

"And you're not," she responded.

Jack ripped the papers in half and let them flutter to the floor. "Do you remember asking me why I didn't walk away when you didn't get pregnant the first time? And I told you that a promise was a promise and a deal was a deal? I've come to claim what's mine, Maddie. That contract won't stand up in court and we both know it."

Jack heard her suck in a sharp breath before a low keening noise filled the room. She dropped to her knees, wrapped her arms around her middle and sobbed uncontrollably. He rushed to kneel at her side, mentally kicking himself for going on the attack. If he'd caused harm to her or the baby, he'd never forgive himself.

"Tell me where it hurts, sweetheart. I'll call 911 and tell them to meet us at the highway."

Maddie unwrapped her arms and slapped at him. "Get away from me." She hiccupped and inched away. "I swear I'll…I'll fight you with everything I have. There is no way you'll take this baby away and use it—"

Jack grasped her arms and held them still. "No, Maddie. You don't understand."

"I understand all right." She squirmed in his grasp. "I see it every day. Parents too wrapped up in their own drama to see they're hurting their child. You forget I'm an attorney and you're just a…a…"

"A what? An SOB? I'll give you that one. What else?" he demanded. "A former juvenile delinquent? Business owner? Grieving friend? The man who loves you so damn much it hurts?"

Jack saw her eyes widen in astonishment.

"You…you love me?"

He nodded mutely.

Jack released her arms and held her face between his hands. "Maddie, sweetheart. Listen to me." He tilted her face so their gazes met. "I want it all—you, the baby, midnight feedings, carpools, Little League, dance recitals." He pressed his lips to hers and kissed her tenderly.

"All of it?" She swallowed hard then hiccupped again.

"All of it."

* * *

"Just a little to the left. There. It's perfect." Maddie directed two men positioning the king-size bed they'd moved from the basement to the master bedroom. Jack's plaid duvet had been replaced with one in a mix of green, cream and burgundy florals and stripes.

"Coming through." Jack entered, carrying a sturdy rocking chair he'd insisted on purchasing even though Maddie was only a few weeks pregnant. He placed it in the corner, and motioned for Maddie to sit. "Go ahead. Give it a test drive." He nudged one of the runners and set the chair in motion.

"Where do you want me to put this, boss?" One of Jack's foremen pointed to the upholstered chair the rocker had replaced.

"Put it in the basement with the rest of the furniture we moved out of here."

"Sure thing. That's a nice space. Your kid'll be having sleepovers down there before you know it."

Jack groaned and flopped backward onto the mattress.

"Worrying about your past coming back to haunt you in the form of a junior version of yourself?" Maddie bit her lip to keep from laughing.

"Don't remind me. If any of our daughter's boyfriends are like me, I'll have to stand guard at the door with a shotgun."

"What if it's a boy?" Maddie patted her still-flat abdomen.

"Then look out world because Jack Jr. will be hell on wheels." He sat upright and pushed off the bed. "I need to help the guys load the stuff we're taking to the women's shelter."

"I can help with that. I'm not a hot-house flower."

Jack placed his hand over hers. "True, but this little one is. You've done plenty. Rest. And that's an order," he said when she opened her mouth to argue.

"But—"

Jack stopped her with a kiss, and her argument vanished.

"I love you," she called out as he left the room. She set the rocker in motion again and surveyed the changes to the master bedroom—new colors, new furniture, new everything including a new life with Jack.

The promise holding them together was the one to love, honor and cherish.

Forever.

Epilogue

A thin whimper interrupted Jack's dream of making love to his wife on a houseboat in the middle of Lake Lanier under a moonless sky. As the cry intensified, he remembered the newest addition to the family—the one whose cry came from the cradle beside his and Maddie's bed.

Maddie shifted beside him, mumbling incoherently. The last month of her pregnancy had coincided with a brutal Atlanta heat wave that left her with swollen ankles and the disposition of an angry camel.

"I'll get it," he said, shoving the covers aside and sitting up on the side of the bed. "You just get ready to nurse." He shoved his feet into a pair of slippers and adjusted the drawstring on his sleep pants.

By the time he'd turned on a low-wattage lamp and reached the cradle, the cry was a full-bore wail. He patted the dark-haired baby on the tummy and began to unsnap the tiny sleeper.

"Hungry, are you?" he asked as he gently pulled the baby's chubby legs from the garment. "I'll get you to your mama in a minute. Bet you'd like some dry britches first, huh?"

He efficiently swapped the soggy diaper for a fresh one, and when the sleeper was back in place he scooped the baby up and against his shoulder.

In two strides he was beside the bed where Maddie had pushed herself up against the burled wood headboard with a pillow behind her back and a U-shaped pillow on her lap.

He watched in silence as Maddie positioned the baby at her breast. The tiny mouth rooted for her nipple before latching on and feeding greedily.

"Remind me to thank Suzanne for this nursing cushion the next time we see her," she said, tapping the fabric that coordinated with the bedding

"It's amazing," Jack whispered.

"Not really. Mothers around the world do this."

"I mean the whole thing. You, me, a baby."

Maddie smiled at him. "Yeah, you are pretty amazing."

Jack crawled back onto the bed and propped on his side to continue watching the baby feast at Maddie's breast. Movement in the hallway outside their bedroom caught his attention.

"Can I sweep wif you, Daddy?"

A little girl with sleep-tousled blonde curls and wearing pink flowered pajamas stood in the doorway. She held a well-loved stuffed bunny in one hand and a much newer teddy bear in the other. A ragged blanket hung around her neck.

Jack looked at Maddie, raised one eyebrow and waited for her answer. At her nod, he patted the bed beside him.

"Sure, Lily, but you have to be very still and very quiet so you don't bother your sister."

The child climbed onto the bed, positioned her bunny and bear and snuggled beside Jack with the blanket between them. He breathed in the fragrance of baby soap and kissed his daughter softly on top of her head.

"Let me know when Grace finishes nursing and I'll put her back in the cradle for you," he whispered.

"I'll do it. You have your hands full with Lily and her menagerie."

Maddie, Lily and now Grace.

The transition from confirmed bachelor to family man had been rocky at times, but Jack couldn't imagine himself living any other way now. Maddie was the love of a lifetime and Lily kept him entertained and amazed on a daily basis.

Lily shifted beside him until her mouth was beside his ear. "I wuv you, Daddy," she said in a loud whisper.

His heart stuttered in his chest at the simple statement. He would never tire of hearing those words. His ability to love grew every day, and he didn't question it at all. The love of his wife and daughters sustained him more than he had ever imagined possible.

"I wuv you too, baby." Jack rubbed noses with his older daughter, their special method of showing affection. He tucked the sheet around them and she popped her thumb in her mouth while fingering the silky binding on her blanket.

"Daddy wuvs all his girls."

ABOUT THE AUTHOR

In 2001, Marilyn discovered romance novels quite by accident, which led to a renewed interest in writing. She's had over forty stories published in the confessions and romance magazines and taught a class in how to effectively write for this genre. She is a member of Romance Writers of America and her local RWA chapter, Heart of Dixie Romance Writers. Her involvement on the local and national levels has combined to give her a great love of the romance genre and to develop friendships that span the globe.

In addition to reading and writing, Marilyn loves to knit simple things, cook in the crockpot and garden in a few pots on her patio. Her motto is "Have passport, will travel," and she recently added Ireland and Wales to the list of 32 states and 21 foreign countries she has visited.

A native of North Carolina, she came to Huntsville, Alabama by way of Frankfurt, Germany. She has lived there longer than anywhere else and calls it home. After raising two great sons, she loves to dote on her two granddaughters. And somewhere amidst all the above, she fits in a day job as an administrative assistant for a boutique law firm.

Did you enjoy this book? Drop us a line and say so! We love to hear from readers, and so do our authors. To connect, visit www.boroughspublishinggroup.com online, send comments directly to info@boroughspublishinggroup.com, or friend us on Facebook and Twitter. And be sure to check back regularly for contests and new releases in your favorite subgenres of romance!

Are you an aspiring writer? Check out www.boroughspublishinggroup.com/submit and see if we can help you make your dreams come true.

www.ingramcontent.com/pod-product-compliance
Lightning Source LLC
Chambersburg PA
CBHW071245130626
46556CB00003B/1173